THE
BUTTON
WAR

THE
BUTTON
WAR

AVI

WALKER
BOOKS

First published in Great Britain 2018 by Walker Books Ltd
87 Vauxhall Walk, London SE11 5HJ

2 4 6 8 10 9 7 5 3 1

Text copyright © 2018 Avi Wortis, Inc.
Cover illustration © 2018 David Dean

The right of Avi Wortis, Inc. to be identified as author of this
work has been asserted by him in accordance with the
Copyright, Designs and Patents Act 1988

This book has been typeset in Ashley Script,
Duckling and ITC Slimbach

Printed and bound by CPI Group (UK) Ltd, Croydon CR0 4YY

British Library Cataloguing in Publication Data:
a catalogue record for this book is
available from the British Library

ISBN 978-1-4063-8083-5

www.walker.co.uk

For Lisa Hartman and Ed Stein

AUGUST 1914

1

The forest was quiet. The August heat had made the air soft, ripe with the smell of earth and growing things. Tall, old trees arched over us like an ancient church. Here and there, rays of sun poked down to dot plants with specks of light. A few small white and blue flowers showed shy faces while an occasional mushroom had popped up from the ground, like a moist brown bubble.

Animals were there – red deer, foxes, martens, snakes. Not that we saw or heard them. Our constant jabber and laughter would have chased anything away.

There were seven of us: Drugi, Jurek, Makary, Raclaw, Ulryk, Wojtex and me, Patryk – all eleven or twelve years old. Nothing like a club or a gang – more like a flock of wild goats. We'd race around our village, roam nearby fields, steal some fruit, kick an old ball up and down the street, play hiding games or dash in and out of one another's homes to share news, such as "Wojtex's sister cut her finger!"

We even dressed pretty much the same: baggy trousers, dark shirts, cloth caps, plus old shoes or patched boots. Of course, there were differences. Raclaw, whose father was well off, wore mostly new clothes with jet buttons. Jurek, at the other end of things, seemed to keep his clothing together with bent pins.

Didn't seem to matter. We seven always did things together. That's why when Jurek said he was going to the ruins because his sister was mad at him and had told him to get out of her house, we went with him. "Anyway," he said, "that's my real home."

About a mile into the forest, we left the road – Jurek in the lead – and tramped under the dark trees until we reached higher ground. That's when we saw collapsed foundations and fragments of old walls, the stones mottled green-grey with moss and lichens. Most of it was half sunk in the earth. There was also a crooked chimney with a usable hearth.

I thought that it had once been a farm.

Makary was sure the place was an abandoned bandits' hideout.

Ulryk believed it was an old church.

Jurek insisted the ruins had been a castle, which had belonged to the ancient Polish king Bolesław the Brave. What's more, Jurek claimed he was the true descendent of Bolesław, so *he* was the real owner of the ruins, the forest, and even our village.

Knowing Jurek had invented the story to make himself feel important, we treated his notion for what it was, a joke. Jurek was no more royal than he was the man in the moon. Other kids in the village may have been as poor as Jurek; I didn't know them.

When we got to the ruins, we did what we always did: set out to collect wood to make a fire in the hearth. It didn't matter that the day was warm. Sitting in front of a fire made us feel as if we were having an adventure.

Jurek and I went off together, walking side by side, looking for wood.

"Your sister going to let you back home?" I asked.

"She always does," he said with a shrug and grin to tell me he didn't care.

As we were grabbing sticks, I saw something small sticking out of the dirt. I bent over and picked it up.

"Let me see," cried Jurek. "I saw it first," not that

he had. I swung around, my back to him, even as I brought the small thing close to my eyes.

"What is it?" said Jurek. "What?"

As far as I could tell, it was just a plain old rusty button.

"Is it money?" demanded Jurek. "A jewel?"

"Button."

"I need it."

I looked at him. "No, you don't. You use pins."

That shut him like a slammed door. He stood there, mouth open a bit, face puke pale. In fact, he looked so stupid, I laughed.

My laugh was like a trigger. He lunged forward and tried to snatch the button. "Belongs to me!" he cried.

"Doesn't," I said, evading him.

"Does. The whole forest belongs to *me*." He was dancing around, trying to get the button.

I kept shifting so he couldn't.

"Come on!" he yelled. "It's mine!"

I stepped away and looked at him. He was breathing hard, his hands were balled into fists, and his cheeks were red. I'd never seen him so angry. I said, "What's the matter with you?"

"Everything on this land is *mine*!" he shouted. "Give it. I'm king here!"

"That's so stupid."

"Isn't!" he screamed, and made another grab, but I twisted away.

I'll admit: I had no use for the dumb button. As far as I was concerned, Jurek was acting stupid because of that King Bolesław story. It made me not want to give him the button.

Next moment, he snatched a big stick from the ground and lifted it high, as if about to bring it down on me. "Give!" he roared, face full of rage. He was waving that stick around like a club.

Suddenly scared, I retreated a few steps and stared at him, unable to understand what was happening.

"I'm warning you!" he cried, and came closer, the stick hovering. "Everything on this land is *mine*. All of it! Give!"

My heart was thumping, but I didn't want to back off.

"Fine," I said, and threw the button as far away as I could. "You want it, get it."

He didn't even glance where I had thrown it. He just stood there, holding up that stick, panting, trembling. I couldn't believe the hate I saw on his face.

He lowered the stick gradually but kept glaring at me.

I found my voice. "I'm going back," I said, and ran off, leaving Jurek where he was, gripping the stick, still furious.

When I got to the ruins, I didn't say anything to the others. It was all too creepy. And senseless.

After a while, Jurek returned. He seemed calm, though at first he wouldn't look at me. Or say anything. And I didn't ask him if he had found the button. Or why he had acted so insane. Instead, we all sat by the fire the way we always did, talking, fooling around.

When it began to get dark, we got up, prepared to go home. Jurek held back.

Trying to smooth things over, trying to be nice, I called, "You coming home?"

He looked at me, his face a blank. "This is my home," he said.

We went off. He stayed.

As I walked back to the village, I kept thinking about what had happened. The truth is, I'd never seen such hatred on anyone's face as I'd seen on Jurek's. Baffled, I tried to forget his craziness, hoping it wouldn't happen again.

But it did.

2

When I think about it now, I guess Jurek and I were like two dogs in the same pack. Sometimes we'd circle each other and wag our tails. Other times we'd snarl and threaten each other, the way we did in the ruins. In other words, we were friends, you might say even best friends, but at the same time, rivals. Not that he and I – or anyone else – spoke about it. Or understood why it was that way. It just was what it was.

But if we seven boys had a leader, it was Jurek. He was the one who came up with new ideas about things to do. Living in a small village the way we did, new ideas were hard to come by. He was good at that.

Some of Jurek's schemes were fine: races, fishing contests, fort building. Others were not so nice: toppling Mr Konstanty's ancient apple tree, stuffing the magistrate's house chimney with straw, running away and hiding in the forest for a week without telling anyone. They weren't exactly wicked, but close.

Thing is, we boys were always daring one another to do this or that. But understand, we almost never *did* the bad stuff. Mostly, it was fun to challenge one another, like roosters in a farmyard. Only, instead of crowing, we laughed. Dares were the way we measured one another, tested one another, who was strong, who was weak.

I was the one who usually objected to Jurek's bad ideas, the dares that were *against* someone. I suppose it was because my parents were strict, insisting I tell them what I was doing, and passing judgement. Of course, I didn't tell them *everything*.

It was funny how, though Jurek and I were friends, we were so unalike.

Both twelve years old, but I was taller, bigger.

He had long brown hair, a narrow face, and pale blue eyes.

I had short blond hair, a round face, big ears, and was mostly easygoing.

Jurek was always saying how important he was, that King Bolesław junk. It was the worst when we were at the ruins.

My parents were always telling me I had to take care of people.

Since Jurek's mother and father died a long time ago, he lived with his eighteen-year-old sister. We boys thought she was pretty. He also had another older sister, but she had married and left town. I had no idea where.

The place Jurek and his sister lived was a one-room shack at the end of a narrow alley at the far edge of the village. A tumbledown place.

My parents and I lived in a three-room wooden house on a narrow street near the village centre. There was a main room with my parents' bed, covered with a feather-stuffed quilt, a kitchen with three chairs, a table for eating, plus a glass window. My father had his workshop in the back. Beyond that was an outhouse.

Jurek's sister washed laundry for the Russian soldiers who lived in the old barracks west of town. She used the river to do washing and then hung the uniforms out to dry on a rope strung between trees behind her house. The washing brought her just enough money to pay rent and buy food. But her hands were always red from using lye soap in cold water.

Once the laundry was dry and folded, Jurek brought it to the Russians and brought back dirty clothing. He also collected the pay for his sister, but he didn't always give her the full amount. At least that's what he told me, swearing me to secrecy. But since he was always exaggerating and bragging, I wasn't sure it was true.

My father was a wheelwright, repairing and making wooden wagon wheels. It was what his father and *his* father had done – back, I supposed, since the world began. In fact, my father liked to say, "The world has always rolled on wooden wheels. Always will. Remember that and you'll have a living." So, to learn the skills, I worked in his shop.

In our small kitchen, my mother cooked on a wood-burning stove – me supplying wood and water. There was always an iron pot of soup that never cooled or emptied. She also patched farm workers' clothing in exchange for food, which went into that pot. Every night the three of us had supper together. My mother insisted.

Jurek rarely took meals with his sister. The two of them fought a lot, and she was always telling him to go away, like that day when we went to the ruins.

At school I was an OK student. Jurek? Everybody knew he was the worst. I slept on a high, wide wooden shelf in our warm kitchen. To get there, I climbed a ladder my father had built when I was younger.

On that sleeping shelf, I had a small box with a lid that my father made for me when I was confirmed. I kept special things inside it: a piece of silver thread, a butterfly with shimmering green wings, a coloured picture of Saint Adalbert, and a pure white stone, which had a blue streak like a cat's eye.

I don't think Jurek owned anything.

As for that button business at the ruins, I forgot about it, so things went on as they usually did – until something astonishing happened.

3

It was still August, and I was going to school, running down the main street, when I noticed an enormous black bird flying out of the blood-red western sky. It was heading towards my village.

Though the old wooden schoolhouse with its stubby bell tower was only fifty yards away, I stopped and stared, trying to make sense of what I was seeing. I took a glance around to see if any of my friends were about. I didn't see any. But the village was busy, with plenty of people on the street. Mr Kaminski was opening the shutters to his tiny pots and pans store. Mrs Kaczmarek was laying out her used boots. I saw Mr Zajac and his donkey-pulled milk wagon go by. And there were lots more, such as the farmworkers walking out to the fields that surrounded the village. But no one seemed to have noticed that big bird but me.

After a few minutes of staring at the bird – if that's what it was – I realized it had *double* wings, one over the other. That wasn't like any bird I'd ever seen before. Made me think it wasn't a bird but a gigantic insect, something like a dragonfly, with its multiple wings. To see such an enormous one would be amazing; in my village, I didn't get to see unusual things very often.

As I stood there, gawking, I noticed that the wings on this creature weren't moving. Was it a raven soaring on the wind? But there was no wind and the hot, humid air was already as limp as a dead fish in Mrs Zielinski's fish store.

Then I began to hear a steady beating sound that seemed to come from this flying thing. Wasn't a buzzing or humming noise, nothing like a bumblebee, or mosquito; more a *clatter-clatter*. Made me think of grasshopper wings. The only other sound I could think of was an axe banging – *crack, crack, crack* – very fast. Of course I knew that whatever it was, it couldn't be an axe up there.

Now a few people did turn and look up, but they

didn't *do* anything other than stare for a moment before going about their business.

I stood there, fascinated.

Whatever the *thing* was, it dropped lower until it was about three hundred feet above the ground. Even so, it continued to fly on, drawing nearer to where I was standing.

More people on the street stopped whatever they were doing and, like me, watched it.

Then I realized that there were wires and sticks on those double wings, as well as what looked like smoke flowing out from what I supposed was its nose. It was almost as if it were a fire-breathing flying dragon. Except I didn't believe in dragons.

Then I saw something like a grey disc in front of this thing's nose – if it was a nose. It seemed to be spinning. Maybe, I told myself, I was seeing a *machine*, a machine that could fly. I thought of it because of what Raclaw had told me, that people had invented machines that could fly.

People talked about all kinds of new inventions in what we called the "far world". Things that weren't in our village. Even so, when Raclaw told me about machines that could fly, I didn't believe him.

"How can a machine fly?" I said.

"They just do."

"Where'd you hear about them?"

"From a newspaper my father gets. Tells about things like that. They're called aeroplanes."

"You ever see one of those ... aeroplanes?" I found it hard to say the word.

"Just a picture."

"Well, then, I don't believe you."

"Don't care if you do or don't. It's true."

As I stood there watching, I began to think that Raclaw might have been right, that I *was* seeing a flying machine.

Behind the machine's nose was a bump, which, after more staring, I realized was a man sitting *in* the machine. The man's head was huge, with round, shiny eyes that didn't seem human. If anything was an insect, he was. Which was strange. Unsettling.

I looked around to see if anyone was acting fearful. Although a lot of people were now looking, no one seemed alarmed.

With a burst of speed, and loud *clatter-clatter*, the aeroplane – if that's what it was – flew over my head so that I had to lean way back to see how big it was. When it went by, a black shadow passed over the village. Now *everyone* on the street stopped whatever they were doing and gawked. People were even peering out of open windows.

The aeroplane flew past me, whipping up a whirl of wind. As it did, I saw black crosses on its wings, plus wheels and some kind of mechanical tail, so that I decided it really was one of those flying machines. I was thrilled.

Next moment, I saw something drop from it. My first thought was that it was a part of the machine or (still thinking of birds) an egg. Wanting to grab it, I started to run towards where I thought it had fallen.

Then there was a red flash, followed by a huge explosion. In less than a second, plumes of yellow, blue and red flames burst from the schoolhouse.

4

The force of the explosion punched me hard in the chest, staggering me. Even so, I managed to stay on my feet and stare at the school. It was engulfed in flames, with dense black smoke pluming into the air. There was a sour stench too, something that stung my eyes. I looked for the flying machine. It had soared high into the sky, turned a wide circle, and was now heading back in the direction from which it had come, the west.

Next moment, panicky people – shouting, crying, screaming – were racing towards the burning school.

The building right next to the school was the church. People – mostly women – were pouring out of it, too, including our old priest, Father Stanislaw.

There were also Russian soldiers running from the village barracks, some with rifles in their hands.

I ran towards the school but stopped when I saw two kids, then four, stagger out of the flaming front door of the schoolhouse. I recognized one of them as a nine-year-old boy named Cyril. His clothing was on fire, and he was screaming as I had never heard anyone scream before.

As I watched, horrified, Cyril fell to the ground and began to thrash about. Father Stanislaw ran to him and tried to beat out the flames with his bare hands. It didn't help; Cyril continued his awful cries.

More village people – yelling and shouting – rushed by. Some went to Cyril. Others tried to put out the school fire. I was so frightened, I had stopped moving. I was sobbing, too. Couldn't help it.

Within moments, the burning building collapsed with a loud *whooshing* sound, as if someone had sucked in a deep breath and taken the school away.

Numb, I watched as they carried away Cyril, dead. Our teacher, Mr Szujski, also died.

When my panicky mother found me, I was just standing there, still too frightened to move. She hugged me to her heart and kept kissing my forehead. I couldn't stop crying. Neither could she.

Later, still dazed, still trembling, I wandered around and listened to what people were saying. They believed that it *was* an aeroplane and that it had dropped what they called a bomb on the school.

In other words, the flying machine brought war to my village.

5

I was born in the village and lived my whole life there. Wasn't big. Had no more than a hundred or so wood and brick houses. None of those buildings were large, save for the three-storey brick one where the magistrate lived. I suppose a thousand people lived there, almost all poor. Yes, there were a couple of rich landlords, but most people were farmers and peasants who worked small fields, which surrounded the village. There were some shop owners, too, but they made very little money.

We had a main street paved with stones in the village centre. Threading from the centre were narrow, twisting side streets and alleys. Being dirt, they became deep with mud in wet weather, muddy brown slush in winter.

In the surrounding fields, potatoes, cabbages, onions and rye grew. Beyond that, a couple of miles to the east, was the thick forest, green and dark in summer, grey and white in winter.

In the middle of the village was a river, which we just called the River. Half the people lived on the east side of the River, the other half on the west side, but we were one village. A rickety wooden bridge spanned the water. People said the bridge was the reason our village was built.

The River water was cold. Like Jurek's sister, people washed clothes in it. In the summer, my friends and I swam or fished in it. In winter, even when it snowed, the River never froze. It flowed too fast, as if it wanted to get away from us.

There was also a Catholic church, Saint Adalbert's, with our old priest, Father Stanislaw. I liked him. He didn't scold and he told good stories.

Behind the church was a crowded cemetery, so even when villagers died, they didn't go away.

Before the aeroplane bombed it, we had a school, a building with one room. None of us liked going. It was boring and the teacher, Mr Szujski, had a wooden cane with which he liked to whack our shins when we gave wrong answers, which according to him was most of the time. Jurek got hit more than anyone. Also, by government decree, Mr Szujski taught only in Russian. No one was allowed to speak Polish in school.

The one road that led in and out of town had been made with grey-white clay. At night, if the moon was bright, it sparkled like an earthbound Milky Way. Mr Wygoda, the village's barrel maker, and my father's friend, once told me that if I walked west on the road long enough, I would come to a large city. He also said that if I did the same going east, there'd be an even bigger city. I never asked their names.

Sometimes I had the notion that I might like to walk the road, east or west. But since I didn't know where I'd end up, I accepted that I lived in the middle of nowhere, that I would stay in the village for the rest of my life – and death – like everyone else.

We used to joke that nothing had changed in our village for a thousand years and nothing would for the next thousand. That's why the coming of the aeroplane and the dropping of the bomb was so huge. For the first time in my life, I didn't know what was going to happen.

No one did.

In the middle of the village, on our main street, close to the bridge, was a three-foot-high cement platform, about ten feet by ten feet. Built on top of it was a water pump with large wheels on either side of a rusty iron tap. Turn the wheels and good, cold water flowed out. As far as I knew, it had been there for ever.

Mornings and early evenings, families gathered there with wooden buckets for their daily supply of water. That was one of my family jobs.

In the afternoons, women came for cooking water

and to exchange news. After dinner, men went to the tavern just across the way to sit on the benches and exchange their version of the news. Opposite the pump was the magistrate's house. Most evenings – especially in the heat of summer – my six friends and I gathered at the pump.

There were other kids in the village, lots, but as far as we were concerned, that pump platform was *ours*. If we boys were in place, we made certain it was just us.

Every evening – late, too, when it was hot – after school, chores or work were done, we boys got on that platform and sat in our space and watched people, wagons, carts, and horses as well as donkeys go by. We gathered at the pump so often that villagers called it "The Fountain of Youth".

Sitting there, we told bad jokes, said stupid things, laughed, kicked our feet, hooted at girls, punched one another's shoulders for no reason – and talked, our words fluttering over one another like a pack of cards being constantly shuffled.

Three days after the bomb was dropped, we boys were at the pump in the afternoon because we had just attended Cyril's funeral. He'd been so badly burned, he was completely covered up. Father Stanislaw told

Ulryk that Cyril didn't have a face anymore.

To hear it turned my stomach.

During the funeral, we knew we were supposed to be sorrowful, so we tried to act properly. But the service was long and we didn't know how to deal with all the grief. It was hot August weather, and the tears and pain smothered us like a thick quilt.

Sitting on the hard church pews, we kept stealing looks at one another, making faces, ducking heads, scratching itchy legs until finally, when someone in the congregation belched, we had to work hard to keep from laughing.

After the burial, people in the village stood in front of the church and talked about whether or not the aeroplane would come back and drop another bomb.

At the pump, we didn't talk about Cyril, either. Though sad and upset, we didn't know how to talk about him or our teacher. Not even the fact that the schoolhouse had become a blackened ruin was something we could talk about. The truth was, it was fine with us that we had no more school. As I said, we hated the teacher, Mr Szujski. The truth is, all we could talk about was why that aeroplane had come and dropped the bomb on us.

And – would it come back?

7

"What I don't understand," said Makary, "is how come, since there's nothing in this village, a war came here." Makary was small for his age, but our fastest runner. Always bouncy, he had trouble sitting. He even talked fast.

"Because we're important," said Jurek.

"How?" asked Raclaw.

We teased Raclaw because he wore lopsided wire eyeglasses, which he claimed he needed to read books, the only one of us who did. His father had lots of Polish, Russian and German books. He could read them, too. Raclaw's father was the village lawyer and also head of the School Committee, so Raclaw never got caned.

Jurek – who got caned in school more than anyone – thumped himself on the chest. "Why is the village important? Because I live here and I'm the descendent of King Bolesław. That's why they dropped all those bombs."

"Just one bomb," I said. I had the right to say that because among my friends, I was the one who saw it happen. My problem was I couldn't get the sound of the aeroplane, that *clatter-clatter,* out of my head. That noise had become stuck inside me. I knew why, too: I was scared it would come back. Of course I kept my fears to myself. If we boys had one rule, it was never admit to being scared. Otherwise, none of us could have lived with all the dares we threw at one another.

"That aeroplane was from Germany," said Jurek with absolute certainty.

"But my father," said Wojtex, "says Russia owns us." Wojtex was a fat boy who lived on pork sausages and believed – and repeated – everything his father, the village butcher, told him. He never had his own ideas. And he waddled when he walked.

"What's the difference between Russia and Germany?" asked Drugi.

Drugi was the smallest, a frail kid who was for ever asking questions, always trying to understand things, never quite getting it right. We let him hang around, almost like a good-luck charm, and while we made fun of him, we didn't let other kids tease him.

After a few moments of silence, during which no one answered Drugi's question, he asked another: "What country are *we* in?"

"We're Poland," said Wojtex. "That's what my father says."

Makary shook his head. "But we're called Galicia."

"Except Russia owns us, right?" I said.

"I own it," said Jurek.

"How can you *own* a country?" said Drugi.

"Russia does," said Raclaw. "I read about it. They've been here since 1795."

"And *they* call us Vistula," agreed Makary.

"But that's wrong," said Raclaw, adjusting his glasses. "This is Poland. But like I said, we're not our own country."

Drugi said, "What's that mean?"

"Russia runs everything," said Raclaw.

Drugi said, "Is that why Russian soldiers are here?"

Jurek said, "It's because my ancestor King Bolesław invited them."

I said, "Someday I hope this King Bolesław shows up and tells you what an idiot you are."

Laughter, though Jurek flipped me a dirty look.

After a moment, Ulryk said, "Father Stanislaw says the Russians are here because they want us to switch to their religion." Six months ago, Ulryk had announced that he was going to become a priest. He already was an altar boy and seemed to get churchier

33

every day. Usually, when he spoke, it was something connected to religion.

Makary said, "No: they're here to teach us the Russian language."

We hooted again. It was true; most people in the village spoke Russian as well as Polish.

Jurek said, "I should be the king around here."

I said, "If you were, I'd start a revolution."

That brought jeers.

Wojtex said, "All I want to know is, will there be more war here?"

"Has to be," said Jurek. "Once you start a war, it can't just stop. Got to be more killing. That's what war is about."

"Will it have anything to do with us?" Drugi asked, looking worried.

Ulryk said, "It's against religion to kill anyone."

"If I didn't like someone, I'd kill him," bragged Jurek.

Makary said, "You hated Szujski, but you never did anything."

"True: I should have grabbed his cane and beaten him to death."

Remembering Jurek's fury in the forest, I thought, *Maybe he would kill someone.*

"Killing is against the law," said Raclaw.

Next moment, Wojtex said, "My father told me that more Russian soldiers are coming. Maybe Cossacks."

Jurek said, "Love to see them."

"Why?" asked Drugi.

Jurek said, "They're the best fighters in the world."

Drugi asked, "Who are the Russians going to fight?"

"Germans," said Wojtex.

Ulryk said, "There are no Germans here."

"Will be," said Raclaw. "My father said so."

There was a moment of silence. After which Drugi asked, "What's the war about?"

We were silent. No one knew the answer.

8

Ulryk said, "The bomb that hit the school was meant for the church right next door."

Wojtex nodded. "My father said the aeroplane flyer confused the two."

"How could he do that?" asked Drugi.

"You ask too many stupid questions," shouted

Jurek, and he punched Drugi's shoulder, knocking him off the pump platform. Drugi, who was used to being treated that way, said nothing, just grinned and climbed back on.

"It's because both buildings have steeples," said Makary.

Ulryk said, "It's an awful sin to bomb a church."

"According to you," said Jurek, "everything is a sin."

"God makes the rules. Not me."

"Kings make the rules," said Jurek, and gave himself a thump on his chest.

"Isn't it a sin to bomb anything?" asked Drugi.

Makary said, "Cyril's mother has gone crazy with her one kid being killed."

Ulryk said, "Father Stanislaw says that when war comes, women cry."

Remembering that I had cried when I saw Cyril on fire, I stared at my feet.

Jurek jumped off the platform. "I'm going home. The only one who'd kill me is my sister. I have to deliver her laundry."

"Where?"

"The Russian barrack."

"Don't talk German!" called Raclaw.

"That's your problem, not mine," returned Jurek. He took two steps away but turned to look at me. "Need to talk to you," he said.

Puzzled, but curious, I got up. "See you guys."

"So long."

"Nice funeral!" said Jurek.

"It's a sin to joke about death," shouted Ulryk.

Jurek lifted his hand and snapped his fingers. "That's what I care about death!" he yelled back.

Everyone laughed as we walked away. But I was wondering what Jurek had to talk to me about.

As Jurek and I walked down the street, I kept glancing at him, waiting for him to say something. But as we went along, he kept checking over his shoulder to make sure we were alone. Only after a while did he stop, dig into his pocket, and pull out a clenched fist.

"Want to see something amazing?" he said.

"What?"

"You love buttons, right?"

"Why would you say that?"

"The other day – that time when we went to the ruins... Hold out your hand."

Surprised that he'd talked about what happened, I did as he asked.

Jurek stuck out his fist but kept it closed. "You're the only one I'm showing this to."

"OK."

"Can't tell anyone."

"I won't."

"I'd get into trouble."

"Just show me!"

He dropped a button into my palm.

I peered at it. "This the button I found in the forest?" I asked.

He shook his head. "Better. Look at it."

I brought the button near my eyes. When I did, I saw that a design had been stamped on it: a bird with two heads with wings spread wide. There were also two stretched-out claws under the wings. One claw held some kind of stick, or maybe a sword. Hard to tell. The other claw held a ball with a cross on top. In the middle of the bird was something so small I couldn't tell what it was. It wasn't at all like the plain one I had found in the forest.

"What kind of bird has two heads?" I asked.

"Russian."

"No bird has two heads."

"It's from a Russian uniform. Lot better," said Jurek, "than the button we found."

Ignoring that "we", I said, "You even look at it?"

All he replied was, "This one has a picture of a knight on a horse killing a dragon."

"You're kidding."

"Look at the middle of the bird." He handed me a small magnifying glass. "With this."

"Where'd you get that?"

"Mr Nowak."

"He loan it to you?"

Jurek said nothing. Just smirked.

"You stole it."

"I'll give it back."

I used the magnifying glass to peer at the button. When I did, I saw a tiny dragon. Right away, I wished I had a button like that.

"How'd you get it?" I said.

"I was looking at the uniforms my sister was going to wash. Wasn't thinking anything, but all of sudden she said, 'You'll get a beating if you touch those buttons.'

"You know me. Give me a dare and I'll do it. Last night she had the uniforms hanging on the drying line behind the house." He laughed. "So I cut the button off."

"Just because she told you not to?"

Jurek nodded. "Had to be careful. My sister doesn't like me." He made it sound as if he was proud.

"You're a thief," I said, but continued to study the button. It *was* amazing.

Jurek said, "I'm the only kid who has one. But you'd like one, wouldn't you?"

I knew exactly what he was doing: giving me a dare. After a moment, I said, "Could I get one?"

"You'd have to do it the way I did, secret."

"Sure."

"And at night," he said.

"What about tonight?" I said.

"Can't do it without me."

"OK."

"And you can't tell anyone. Bad things might happen."

"Your sister?"

"The Russians."

"I'm not stupid."

"Bring a sharp knife. We'll go behind my house.

40

That's where my sister hangs the uniforms. Meet me at the bridge after it gets dark."

I gave him back his button and said, "I'll be there."

Jurek made a fist around the button and held it in front of my face. "Admit it: my button is a lot better than that other one."

"How come you always have to be best?"

"Makes me feel good."

"You feel bad that much?"

"If you were a king and nobody noticed, you'd feel bad, too."

I looked at him. "You really believe all that King Bolesław stuff?"

"It's true," he said.

Not wanting to argue, I walked off.

"Don't forget," Jurek called after me, "I got this one first! Which means I'm in charge."

Did I want a Russian button? Well, no. Except, well, yes. There was something about the way Jurek made his dares: if you didn't accept, his brag stood. Then he gloated. Made me want to prove I could be as good as him. And to shut him up.

10

I waited until night. When I was ready to leave, I went to my father. He was in his bedroom reading a wrinkled newspaper by the yellow light of a small lamp. I wondered where he got a newspaper. They were hard to find.

"Have to see Jurek," I said. "Something important. Can I go?"

He didn't look up.

I waited.

Stooped from age and work, he had thin, white hair. His large hands had crooked fingers, big knuckles, blue veins and yellow fingernails. His face and neck were full of lines, and that day, as usual, he hadn't shaved because he saved that for Sunday church.

"How come you're reading?" I asked. He didn't read very often, saying he needed to save his eyes for his work.

He said, "I'm trying to learn about this war."

"Is more coming?"

He shook the paper with both hands, as if an answer might fall out. "I'm trying to find out."

"If it comes, will it make things different?"

"Probably."

"What would happen?"

My father looked at me. "The Russians stagger out of the tavern drunk and beat up a villager. Not for any reason. If anyone complains, our magistrate, Mr Stawska, says, 'Soldiers are soldiers.' Just know the Germans will be no more our friends than the Russians. I've told you what my father always used to say."

Having heard the old saying a million times, I repeated it: "The far world can't be bothered to stoop and talk to the near world. You have to listen for yourself."

"Still true," said my father. He returned to his newspaper.

"May I ask something else?"

"Of course."

"One of my friends always tries to get us to do things that are not so good."

"Jurek?"

I nodded. "Wants to be in charge."

"Among your friends, you're the biggest, aren't you?"

"Suppose."

"And you're strong?"

"I'd … I'd like to be."

"Can't be just *like*."

"Why?"

He studied me with his sharp blue eyes. "Why do you think God made you strong?"

I shook my head.

"To help the weak." He turned back to his reading.

I stood there a moment and gazed at him. Sometimes when I asked my father things, it came back like a challenge. I didn't know how to respond.

When he said no more, I went through to the kitchen. My mother was at the table sewing by candlelight. A small, thin woman, she was always complaining of cold – even in summer. A red kerchief covered her thin hair. Her long green dress was formless. She looked up, a worried look on her creased face.

"Where are you going?" she asked.

"The bridge. To meet Jurek."

She pursed her lips. "I'm not fond of him."

"He's all right."

"Don't come back late."

"Won't."

"I'll leave a candle. I can't sleep until I hear you come in."

"I know." I continued into my father's workshop, where there were all kinds of wood pieces and tools. It was easy to find a small, sharp knife.

Using the back door, I stepped out into the dark, hot and humid air. I could smell the growing fields, hear the whirr of insects, see a sky sparked with stars, along with a clear and sharp quarter moon. Next moment, I heard an owl hoot, once, twice. If an owl hooted three times, it meant bad luck was coming, so I waited. When there were no more hoots, I went on.

11

On the main street, light came from inside people's houses, and there wasn't much. Some of the buildings were large, made of brick, and painted white. They looked like huge silent faces.

Most villagers went to bed early, but as I walked, I passed a few people I knew going home. There was Mr Jankowski, the street sweeper. Mr Mazur who sold vegetables from a box. Mrs Baran from the cloth store. They gave me nods and muttered greetings, but nothing much was said.

When I reached the bridge, I leaned on the railing and gazed down into the River. The water appeared black, though here and there specks glimmered, as if bits of moon had fallen into the water. The River also made a gurgling noise, which was like the sound of a warbling bird deep in the forest.

I stared up at the spread of stars. At night, it was sometimes lighter in the sky than in the village. Father Stanislaw once told us that the points of light were angels. When I was younger, I had the notion that Heaven was a lot more crowded with angels than the village was with people. I'd tried to imagine what a village of angels would be like. I couldn't.

But looking at the sky that night made me think about the aeroplane. Soon as I did, the *clatter-clatter* sound came back into my head. Hearing it reminded me of the school exploding. The burst of light. The flames. The children rushing out. Cyril on fire.

Feeling a sudden chill, I shuddered. If you felt cold during a hot summer, it meant the Angel of Death was near.

My head flooded with questions: *What made that aeroplane come to our village? Can it fly at night? Will it come back and drop another bomb? On what? Do the Germans care about us, and what happened? Are more Russians coming? Will a war really come here?*

I was telling myself, *Go home*, when I heard the sound of footsteps. I whirled around.

12

It was Jurek, small candle lamp in hand. I could hear myself wishing he hadn't come.

"Ready?" he called.

I just held up my knife. In the lamplight, it glinted.

He said, "Let's go."

"Where we headed?" I said when it didn't seem as if we were going towards his house.

"My place. We'll make a wide circle. Don't want my sister to see what we're doing."

"Those Russian uniforms still there?"

"Different ones."

I said, "What'll happen if the Russians notice buttons are missing?"

"People always lose buttons."

I said, "My mother has a small box of them."

"Looking in a box is stupid. This is better."

"When I left my house, I heard an owl."

"How many times?"

"Twice."

"Then don't worry. Anyway, it's better when it's a little scary."

I said, "You said something bad would happen if we got caught."

"Just wanted to see if you frighten easy."

I felt I had to say, "I don't."

"We'll see."

We went on, going through crooked alleyways, the sole sound the crunch of our footsteps on the ground.

13

We came up behind Jurek's tiny house, which was no more than a shack. There was a small, shuttered window, through which some flickering light slipped, as if the night had cracks in it. I could make out a rope that went from one tree to another. Hanging from it were seven Russian army long shirts, as they were called. Having seen them on the soldiers around the village, I knew they were greenish brown.

"Made of cotton," Jurek whispered. "For summer."

"Does it matter?"

"Easier to cut off the buttons. My sister says wool thread is tougher." He blew out his candle lamp. "Come on."

We came up to the uniforms. Since they hung between us and the house, we were well hidden.

I asked, "Which ones have the dragon buttons?"

"No idea. Just grab one. Be fast." He pulled a shirt out and I made a snatch, finding it soft and light.

I felt around for buttons but couldn't find any. "Where?"

Jurek reached out. "Here, idiot."

Seeing a row of glossy buttons, I grabbed the closest and pulled, so it stood out from the shirt. I made a sawing motion with the knife until the button dropped into my hand. "Got it."

"Let's go," he said and started running. I followed, clutching the stolen button in my hand.

We didn't stop until we got back to the bridge. Once there, we leaned over the railing and caught our breath.

Jurek said, "Let's see what you got."

With care, I unfolded my fist. There wasn't much light, but when I brought the button close to my eyes, I saw right away that it was different from Jurek's: tin, maybe, and no double-headed bird clutching a sword and ball. No tiny dragon in the middle. Just plain and dull.

"Nothing on it," I said, disappointed.

Jurek took up the button and eyed it. "You're right," he said. "The one I got is better." He was smiling, gloating.

I had this thought: *He fixed it so that I'd get a dull button.*

Before I could say anything, a voice said, "Too hot for you to sleep?"

14

It was Raclaw, his shining lamp making his eyeglasses glow. Right away I wished I had my button back, but didn't want to let him know what Jurek and I had done. Or that Jurek had a better button than me.

Raclaw said, "Why are you guys here? What were you looking at?"

Jurek said, "Even with eyeglasses you can't see anything."

"Drop dead. What was it?"

Jurek said, "A button."

"A what?"

"Said. Button."

"What kind of button?"

"From a Russian uniform," Jurek told him.

Raclaw said, "What's so special about a Russian button?"

"Nothing," I said.

"Must be something. Let me see."

Jurek reached into his pocket, pulled out his button, and handed it to Raclaw. Adjusting his eyeglasses and then his lamp, Raclaw studied it.

Jurek said, "See? A two-headed bird."

"Birds don't have two heads."

"That does. Has a dragon, too."

"Where?"

Jurek reached into his pocket and hauled out that magnifying glass.

Raclaw eyed Jurek for a second, and then used it. He looked up. "This really from a Russian uniform?"

"Told you," said Jurek.

After a moment, Raclaw said, "Where'd you get it?"

Jurek said, "Give it back. It's mine."

Raclaw looked at me. "You have one?"

"Sort of," I said.

Raclaw said. "As good as Jurek's?"

Jurek glanced at me, smirking. To Raclaw, he said, "Give it back."

Raclaw handed Jurek his button.

The three of us stared down into the River.

To Jurek, Raclaw said, "Your sister washes the Russians' uniforms. And you're always stealing stuff."

"So what?"

"Bet that's where you got the button. You stole it from her laundry."

"Takes guts."

"You could get into trouble for that."

"Only if you told," said Jurek. "You going to?"

Raclaw said, "If you help me get one, I won't say anything."

Jurek shook his head.

Raclaw said, "Make a deal: help me get a dragon button, I'll tell you a big secret."

"What secret?" Jurek said.

Raclaw said, "Not saying till I get my own button."

I said, "Where'd you get your secret?"

"My father speaks to important people."

That was true. Raclaw's father, being a lawyer, was a big person in the village.

Jurek said, "Let's hear the secret, then we'll help you get a button."

"Swear you will," said Raclaw.

Jurek made the sign of the cross over his chest and said, "Swear."

Raclaw said, "If you don't keep your swear, you'll either get sued or go to Hell."

"Tell us!" Jurek yelled.

"OK," said Raclaw. "The Russians are leaving tomorrow."

15

"Leaving! Tomorrow!" I cried. "Why?"

"Because the Germans are coming."

"*Here?*" I said.

"Just told you, didn't I?"

I said, "Are the Russians going to fight them?"

"That's what my father asked Dmitrov. You know, the Russian commandant. They're good friends. Guess what Dmitrov said? Said there's nothing worth defending here except the forest."

"What's special about the forest?" I said.

"It belongs to me," said Jurek.

Raclaw said, "You can hide there. OK. You swore. Show me where to get a button."

Jurek hesitated a moment, then pushed off from the bridge railing, and the three of us headed back to his house. As we walked, Jurek slipped my dull button back into my hand. Frustrated, annoyed, I stuffed it in my pocket.

Raclaw began to talk about how, when the Germans came, everything would change.

"What way?" Jurek asked.

"Don't know. Just will. My father says German law and Russian law are different."

"How?" I asked.

"Bet we'll have to learn German. My father knows it." He went on chattering, but I didn't listen. I was trying to think of what I knew about Germans. *Nothing.* Except the aeroplane. The moment I thought that, the *clatter-clatter* came back into my head.

I shivered so hard I had to make tight fists to stop it.

"Keep quiet," Jurek said as we got near to the back of his house.

We crept forward.

"There you are," Jurek whispered. The Russian uniforms were still hanging from the rope.

Raclaw, holding his lamp up, went nearer. "I don't see any buttons."

"Shhh!" Jurek showed him where the buttons were, under a fold of the shirt.

"How do you get them off?"

"You read books, but you're stupid," Jurek said.

I handed Raclaw my knife.

Raclaw cut a button off, gave the knife back to me, held up his lamp, and peered at the button. "Got a dragon," he announced, a big grin on his face.

I was just about to step forward and cut off another button when the shutter of Jurek's house swung open. "Who's there?" came a call. Jurek's sister.

"Go!" Jurek hissed.

16

We ran back to the bridge. Once there, we put our open hands side by side. Holding Raclaw's light close, we compared the three buttons.

"Mine is the best," Jurek said, and held his button in front of Raclaw's face as if to taunt him.

Knowing my button was the worst, I said nothing.

To Jurek, Raclaw said, "Think your sister is going to wash the German uniforms?"

"I don't know."

Not wanting any more of this button business, I stepped away. "Got to go home. See you," I called.

"'Night."

"Yeah."

I looked back. I saw Jurek go one way, Raclaw another. I was upset. *Forget it*, I told myself. *Buttons are nothing.*

Instead, I thought about Raclaw's news that the Russians were leaving, that the Germans were coming. *How many Germans? Are the Russians afraid to fight? What will happen?* I had one good thought: *If the Germans come, they won't bomb us because they won't bomb their own soldiers. We'll be safe.*

Then I thought about Raclaw's question: "Think your sister is going to wash the German uniforms?"

Next moment, I realized something: if I wanted one of those dragon buttons – with the Russians leaving – I'd have to get one right away.

I stopped in the middle of the street, turned around, and made sure I was alone. *This is your last chance to get a dragon button,* I told myself. *Should I? Shouldn't I? Are you strong or weak?* The next thing that came into my head was what Jurek said: "Just wanted to see if you frighten easy."

The owl hooted again. Twice. I waited. There were no more hoots.

"Do the dare," I said aloud. With that, I turned around, gripped the knife, and headed back to Jurek's house.

17

I had no lamp or candle, and since it was so late, there were almost no house lights. What's more, the sky had clouded up, so the stars had gone, making the darkness complete.

I recalled that time when Father Stanislaw told us that the points of light were angels. That made me think: *What if it wasn't just the Russians who were going? What if the angels also went? If they left, would the angels take things with them? Where would they go?* I wished they would stay.

Then I remembered something my father said: "If you stare into the darkness long enough, you'll see some light."

It worked.

It didn't take long before I was behind Jurek's house again. No light was coming from within. I liked the idea that Jurek was inside and had no idea I was outside.

The dark uniforms on the rope made me think of the souls of men – just hanging there. The thought made me shiver – the third time that day. I didn't like doing things alone and wished one of my friends was with me. Reminding myself what Jurek said, that it's better when things are a little scary, I made a cross over my heart.

All the same, as I stood there, the darkness deeper than the silence, I felt fearful and considered going home. But I knew I wanted a good button more than ever and that they were right there in front of me. If I didn't get one, Jurek would say all that "king" junk.

"Saint Adalbert," I whispered, "make me strong. Make it a good one."

Knife in hand, I moved forward, felt about, found a shirt, fumbled for buttons, touched one, and hacked it off. Gripping it, I ran fast, heading for home.

I slipped inside my house. Despite the heat, my parents lay asleep in their front-room bed under the quilt. My mother was snoring. My father was wearing his nightcap.

In the kitchen, a candle burned on the table. I sat down, pulled out my new button, and examined it for the first time. It was a gleaming gold colour with an easy-to-see double-headed eagle. As for the dragon, when I bent close, I saw it clearly. I didn't even need Mr Nowak's magnifying glass.

I was elated. I'd been strong and had the best button.

I put the knife back in my father's workshop, blew out the candle, then climbed the ladder to my sleeping shelf. Once there, I put the button into my box. I couldn't wait to show it to Jurek.

"Thank you, Saint Adalbert. I promise to be strong."

Proud of myself, I soon fell asleep.

But in the middle of the night, the sound of the aeroplane – *clatter-clatter* – came into my head. With a start, I woke trembling, sat up, and listened. When I heard nothing, I realized it had only been a dream.

Next moment, that sound, the aeroplane's *clatter-clatter*, came back into my head. *Is it real?* I wondered. *No, it's just in my head.*

I fumbled into my box and took out my new button. It was real. It wasn't going to change. It was the best. I held it tight, then rolled over and tried to sleep – only to hear the owl hoot. It came three times. I lay there, wide-eyed, scared, sweating, sure something bad was going to happen. After a while, I drifted off to uneasy sleep. I was clutching the button as if my life depended on it.

When I woke in the morning, the day was hot and humid again, the kind of heavy air that made me want to stay on my sleeping shelf and not move. Still holding that button in my sweaty hand, I didn't want to go into my father's shop to start the workday. I missed school, not that I was going to tell anyone.

I pulled over my box, opened it, dropped in the new button, and shut the lid.

"Hey!"

Jurek was right there, looking at me, a big grin on his face. He had stolen into the kitchen and climbed up my ladder to scare me. I don't know if I was scared, but I was startled.

"Hey," he demanded. "What's that box?"

"None of your business."

"Special stuff? That where you keep your stupid button?"

"Why'd you sneak up like that?"

"Thought you'd like to know: the Russians are going!" he leaped down and tore out of the house.

I snatched up my good button, put it into my

pocket, and scrambled out of bed and pulled on my clothes. Poking my head into my father's workshop, I yelled, "The Russians are leaving!" then ran out. My father and mother followed. As word spread through the village, so did almost everyone else.

By the time I reached the main street, it seemed as if the whole village was there. People were gathered in small groups – men, women and kids, talking among themselves. But as if afraid to speak too loud, they were whispering.

I joined my six friends on the pump platform. Jurek had perched himself highest, atop one of the wheels. I studied the western sky, searching for the aeroplane. Seeing nothing but cloudless blue, I shifted my gaze to the street. "Anyone see the Russians yet?" I asked.

Raclaw said, "They're going to march through the village."

"Where they going?" asked Drugi.

"Home, stupid," said Jurek.

I had no idea where the Russians' home was, but I wasn't going to admit it. Instead, I waited for the question I knew Drugi would ask.

Sure enough, he said, "Where's home?"

"Moscow, probably," said Makary.

"Everybody knows that," said Jurek.

After some long, hot minutes of waiting, I heard the sound of a beating drum coming from the western end of the village.

"They're coming!" cried Jurek from his perch.

Though we boys remained on the pump, people rushed to one side of the street or the other. Hand in my pocket, I squeezed my new button, telling myself how smart I'd been to get a great Russian one. Knowing it was better than Jurek's, I couldn't wait to show him.

20

The first of the Russians to appear was the commandant, Dmitrov. I had never seen a noble, but Dmitrov was what I thought one would look like. He was a large, broad-shouldered man, with a proud, expressionless face, and a fierce, frowning moustache of rust colour. Best of all, he had a scar on his left cheek that we boys were sure he got in a duel, a subject of endless debate. It was Jurek who had had the courage to ask him.

"I fell off my horse" was the answer.

That was a disappointment.

Dmitrov was riding his big brown horse, moving down the middle of the street as if in a parade. He was sitting tall in his dark leather saddle, feet in stirrups, toes pointing out, eyes looking straight ahead. A trickle of sweat ran down the side of his jaw.

He was in his regular uniform, a short light-brown jacket with shoulder boards that had three stripes and the number nine on them. There were bright buttons down the front of his jacket. They must have always been there, but I had never noticed them before. The world had become full of buttons.

On Dmitrov's head was a brown cap with a short, stiff visor, pulled low. His shiny black boots almost reached his knees. A rifle was slung on his back, held in place by a leather strap that crossed his chest. On his left hip was a black holster, which held a pistol.

Although everybody in the village knew him, and he knew them – he had been around for three years – he looked neither to the right nor to the left. I wondered if he was glad to be going. If what people said was true – that the Germans were coming – it meant the Russians were retreating. Even so, there was no sense of urgency about the commandant, or his horse. Everything about him suggested calmness.

I wished I could ask him what the war was about.

Maybe I should become a soldier. I'd get to go somewhere, too.

Right behind the commandant was his sergeant, also on a horse. In one hand, this young man was holding a pole from which a Russian flag flapped. The yellow flag had a large image of a double-headed bird, each head with a crown, and another crown atop those. On the bird's breast was the emblem showing a knight spearing a dragon. Just like the buttons.

I reached up and pulled Jurek's foot.

Jurek, understanding, nodded and grinned. I thought again how great it was going to be to show him my new button.

The officers were followed by a double line of about twenty soldiers. They wore their light-brown uniforms, peaked caps, and shirts reaching below waist belts, from which hung a water flask and a closed bag. The Russian soldiers' jackets had a row of buttons down the front. They looked to be tin, like that first button I'd taken. Their boots, calf height, were black. On their backs hung rifles, which had long, sharp-looking bayonets attached to them.

The troops were marching in a double line, their rifles with bayonets suggesting what harm they could do. But because I knew many of the soldiers by name, they didn't seem very fierce.

When the Russian soldiers reached the pump, their double line split, half going to the left, the other half to the right. It was thrilling to be in the middle.

Once on the other side of the pump, the two lines of soldiers joined again. Never breaking stride, they continued on.

As the soldiers passed near the pump, I could see that one soldier's shirt was partway open. Pointing to him, I whispered to Raclaw, "Button missing!"

Raclaw, with a big grin, rolled his eyes, trying to be funny.

The people from the village watched the departing Russians. No one called out, although a few people waved handkerchiefs. There were no shouts of "Farewell!" or "Good luck!" Beyond that, there was the sound of the drum, and the beat of boots on street stones. I thought how some noises make everything else quiet.

The last of the Russians was a drummer, whose snare drum stuck out from his belly. He held a drumstick in each hand and made a steady rattle, matching the beat of the soldiers' boots. It wasn't just the soldiers who marched to his drumming; the horses did, too.

When the soldiers had passed, five horse-pulled wagons went by. The wagons were piled with military equipment, blankets, plus boxes and trunks.

It didn't take long before the Russians were out of sight, the sound of their drum growing fainter. I imagined they would soon reach the forest and be marching under the trees. It would be cooler there.

Once the Russians left the village, people gathered in the middle of the street and watched the last of the wagons go. Talk grew louder, urgent. People were agitated. The talk wasn't about the Russians leaving; it was about the coming of the Germans. I heard someone ask, "What's going to happen to us?" I didn't hear an answer.

We boys just sat there, no one speaking. Then Makary said, "Wonder when the Germans will come."

Raclaw said, "My father says soon."

21

Drugi asked the question that had been asked before: "Will the Germans be bad?"

"My father doesn't think so," said Raclaw.

"Mine does," said Wojtex. "He likes the Russians."

Raclaw said, "My father hates them."

Ulryk put in, "Father Stanislaw always says, 'Old is good. New is bad.'"

"Funny," said Makary. "The Russians were here my whole life. I suppose I'll miss them. Your sister will," he said to Jurek. "Washing uniforms. Think they'll ever come back?"

"Don't care," said Jurek. "I've got something of theirs." He reached into his pocket, pulled out his Russian button, and held it out in the palm of his hand.

The boys pushed together to look at it.

"What is it?" asked Drugi.

"Button from a Russian uniform. See?" said Jurek. "Just like their flag. Has a dragon."

The button was passed from hand to hand.

"How'd you get it?" Ulryk wanted to know.

"Just did," said Jurek with a quick smug look at me.

"Your sister's washing," said Makary.

"You stole it," said Ulryk. He waggled a finger in front of Jurek's face. Jurek slapped it away.

"Anyway," said Raclaw, holding out his hand with

his button, "I've got a better one."

"Let's see!"

As they shared Raclaw's button, Jurek didn't look happy. I waited a few moments, then pulled out my new button. "Yeah, but I got the best one. Look." I held it out.

My button was the brightest.

Startled, Jurek looked at me. "When did you get that?"

Grinning, I said, "Last night."

"After?"

"Yup." Made me feel good that I'd done better than him.

"Dirty dog," said Jurek, and for a moment his face filled with anger, that same anger I'd seen in the forest.

Makary said, "When the Germans come, maybe we can get some of their buttons."

Wojtex said, "Better than the Russian ones."

"Why will they be better?" asked Drugi.

Raclaw shrugged. "What my father says."

The buttons were passed hand to hand. I kept my eyes on Jurek. He kept glaring at me, furious. Pleased with myself, I grinned back.

All of sudden, he cried out, "Wait! Got a great

idea. We'll have a contest! Whoever gets the best button wins. Winner gets to be king. Means everyone has to bow down to him. Best dare ever. Buttons."

"What buttons?" said Drugi, confused as ever.

"Soldier buttons, stupid," an excited Jurek shouted at Drugi. "The Germans are coming, right? You'll see. They'll have buttons on their uniforms."

"Right," said Raclaw. "To keep their pants up."

"Better than the Russian ones," said Jurek.

"The pants?" said Drugi.

Everybody laughed.

"The buttons, idiot!"

"Will they be different?" asked Drugi.

"Of course," said Raclaw. "They're German."

Jurek, becoming even more excited, said, "Everyone agree? Contest for best soldier button." Jurek looked right at me when he said that. His eyes were laughing at me.

"How're we going to judge which is the best?" said Ulryk.

Jurek said, "We'll know."

Drugi had a worried face. "How do we get them?" he asked.

Jurek said, "That's the whole point. Everybody has to find the buttons their own way. Another rule,"

Jurek added. "You can't *ask* for a button. You have to *get* it."

"You mean steal it?" said Ulryk. He looked upset.

"That's up to you."

"Why do you have to steal?" asked Drugi.

"Makes the dare better. We'll be the only people in the whole village that collects buttons. Nobody else will even see them."

Frustrated, I was about to walk away when I began to hear that faint, steady beating sound, the *clatter-clatter*.

Startled, I looked up and around and saw something in the sky coming from the west: "The aeroplane!" I screamed as loud as I could.

22

Everyone on the street stopped and looked to where I was pointing.

"The aeroplane," I shouted. "It's coming back!"

Shrieking and crying, people began to run. Within moments, the street was deserted. But since none of us boys wanted to show we were scared, we stood and watched the oncoming aeroplane.

As the aeroplane drew nearer, ever bigger, the sole sound was that *clatter-clatter* and it was growing louder. Panicked, I wanted to run but didn't.

Drugi whispered, "Is ... is it going to bomb us?"

The other boys looked at me as if I had an answer.

"Don't know," I mumbled.

It was Jurek who shouted, "Head for the school! He won't bomb that again!"

He jumped off the pump and began to run down the main street. The rest of us scrambled to follow.

As I ran, I heard the aeroplane getting closer.

We reached the school and dove in among the charred timbers, broken benches, desks, and the few old books whose pages were like black lace. If you touched one, it became dust.

Hands and arms covered with soot, we crouched in the roofless school, peered up at the sky, and waited.

"Please keep going ... keep going," I whispered to the aeroplane, as if praying.

Ulryk, eyes closed, had his hands clasped in real prayer.

The aeroplane roared over us. Seeing the black

crosses on the underside of the wings, I cringed.

When the aeroplane flew by, we stood to watch where it was going. It was heading east, beyond the village. We remained still, no one speaking, just waiting and listening. Within moments, we heard an explosion.

Raclaw shouted, "They bombed the Russians!"

We leaped out of the schoolhouse wreckage and began to run, not away from the explosion but towards it, wanting to see what had happened.

23

We moved in a close pack along our one road, crossed the bridge over the River, and kept going. We began to spread out with Makary, our fastest runner, in the lead. Wojtex was last, red faced, puffing, his face covered with sweat, straining to keep up. I was in the middle. I was sweating, too.

We got beyond the village where farm fields, none very large, were to either side of us. In the August heat, the brown rye was almost ready for gathering. Leafy cabbage plants and potato plants looked healthy.

Here and there, farmworkers were in the fields. By the time we passed, they had stopped and were leaning on rakes or scythes, looking in the direction we were heading. One of them shouted, "Come back and tell us what happened!"

I scanned the sky ahead for signs like the kind of smoke that had come from the burning schoolhouse. I didn't see any.

Tired from running in the heat, we slowed down but continued on, more spread out. Wojtex had passed Drugi, who kept shouting, "Wait for me! Wait!"

Some hundred yards from where the forest began, Makary, still in the lead, stopped and stood still. He had his hands held out, as if to keep his balance. He was peering down.

The rest of us, winded and dripping in the heat, caught up to him. He was standing on the edge of a big hole. The road went right up to it and then vanished. Fifteen yards on, the other side of the hole, the road reappeared. It was possible to walk around the hole, but there were trees close in. It would be hard for wagons to get by.

At the bottom of the hole lay scattered broken pieces of wood, some big, some small. There was also half of a wheel. Bits of greenish-brown cloth, the colour of the Russian uniforms, were everywhere. There were also rising wisps of smoke which carried a rancid burn smell, enough to make me cover my nose. Worst of all was a half-buried horse's head. The head was bloody and torn, one eye – a sickly bluish white – protruding.

We stood at the edge of the hole and gawked. The horse head made me feel sick.

It was Makary who said, "They must have dropped a bomb here."

It hadn't just destroyed a Russian wagon; it had killed that horse.

No one spoke until Drugi asked, "Why'd they do that?"

Jurek said, "To make sure the Russians don't come back."

Raclaw said, "It's going to keep people in the village from going away, too."

Ulryk said, "Doesn't look like the bomb killed anyone. No blood or body parts."

"Maybe the Russians took the bodies away," said Makary.

"Left the horse," said Wojtex.

"Do animals have souls?" I asked.

Ulryk shook his head.

75

Raclaw said, "Doesn't matter: that's a Russian wagon down there."

Makary said, "Full of clothing bits. Uniforms, maybe."

"Buttons!" cried Jurek, and next moment he scrambled down into the hole.

"Leave it alone!" I shouted.

Didn't matter what I said – the rest followed Jurek. Uncomfortable about being part of the scavenging, I remained above the hole, alone. But they scrabbled around the bottom, picking up bits and pieces of the cloth, looking for buttons.

"Got one!" called Makary. "Double-headed bird!"

Everyone hurried over. Makary held out his hand with a button on it.

Within moments, Wojtex cried, "Me too."

"That's just like mine," said Raclaw.

They kept searching.

It didn't take long before they all had at least one double-headed button. Even Drugi got one. They climbed out of the crater and bunched together to compare buttons. All were just as good as the one I had.

Drugi said, "Who won the contest?"

Jurek said, "No one. Because they're all the same. Have to wait for German buttons."

"Why?" asked Drugi.

"Because they'll be better."

"How we going to get them?" Drugi asked.

"I told you, dumbhead. That's the whole point of the contest. It takes brains."

No one spoke for a while until I said, "I think it's a stupid idea."

Jurek said, "That's because you'll lose."

Ulryk said, "I better tell Father Stanislaw what happened."

"Fine," said Jurek. "But no telling about the button contest."

"Why?" asked Drugi.

"It's just about us, right?" said Jurek. "Whoever wins gets to be button king. Everyone bows to the king. Whack! Whack!" He punched Drugi's arm. Then Jurek looked over to me and said, "Just Patryk is out."

"I didn't say that."

"Did," said Jurek.

Feeling I had to, I muttered, "I'm in."

There were murmurs of agreement, and we all started back along the road, not running this time, but walking.

Drugi clutched his button. Now and again he peeked at it and smiled, as if he knew a secret.

As we walked, I began to think about what had happened; scavenging in a bomb hole for buttons. It wasn't exactly stealing, but it made me feel uncomfortable, as if my friends had done something wrong. And that horse head was awful. I looked up into the sky. There was no aeroplane. But I was sure another would come, sometime.

24

Jurek and I walked side by side. When we were a little separate from the others, Jurek whispered, "I'm glad the Germans are coming."

"Why?"

He took out his Russian buttons. "Because I'm going to get the best button, beat you, and win the contest."

I said, "It's stupid."

"You came back last night to get one."

"So what?"

"Fine with me. I'll laugh when I'm king. Can't wait for you to bow down. I'll make sure you're the first."

"You'll be first," I shot back. "Because I'm going to win."

We went by a few of the farm labourers. "What happened?" one of them called.

Raclaw shouted, "The Germans bombed the road. You can't go anywhere that way."

Back in the village, we wandered around and told people what we had seen. Villagers were upset, but they didn't know what to make of it. Some said the bombing was an accident. Others said it was to keep the village people penned up. Most of the talk was about trying to guess when the Germans might arrive. People were gathered in small groups, talking loud or whispering. We kept hearing the word "Germans".

25

After a while, we went back to the pump platform, sat around and talked about everything that had happened. Didn't take too long before that chatter faded. Then we just sat there, all talked out, and watched people going about their business. Though we knew things had changed, everything looked normal.

It was Raclaw who said, "It's strange not going to school."

No one said anything about that until Makary said, "We should go back to the school wreckage. Maybe we can find stuff."

Soon as he said that, we jumped off the platform and ran to the schoolhouse – or what had been the schoolhouse.

That first time – when we hid in the school because the aeroplane was coming – we had jumped into the rubble. Now we stood at the edge of it and gazed at what had been our schoolhouse. What we saw was a confused bundle of broken things, all partially buried in the collapsed and splintered wooden walls. There was even a piece of the roof. A lot of it was scorched. But I could recognize some things – broken for the most part – like desks and chairs. It was hard to believe we had spent so much time in it and now it was all scrap.

Jurek – who always went first – waded in and pulled out half of a map, its edges singed. It used to be pinned to the wall. Next moment, we were all stumbling about, looking for things.

Wojtex found the Russian dictionary that Mr Szujski made us use to find right spellings. Only half the pages were there.

Drugi found a torn picture of the Russian czar.

"Look what I found," cried Ulryk. He held up Mr Szujski's cane, the one he used to hit us with when we got the answers wrong. Amid all that wreckage, it had remained whole.

We stopped our searching and stared. That cane was something we hated, feared. It reminded me of Mr Szujski, who was so mean. Only he had been killed. To see it in Ulryk's hand was disturbing.

Suddenly Jurek shouted, "That's what the button king should get: the cane!"

Raclaw said, "Right. Like a sceptre."

"What's a sceptre?" asked Drugi.

I said, "It's what a king holds to prove he's king."

"Right!" cried Jurek. "The perfect contest prize." Next moment, he scrambled forward, snatched the cane from Ulryk's hand, and began to swing it about.

"You going to hit us with it?" asked Drugi, who was standing next to him.

"Maybe," said Jurek, his big grin announcing how pleased with himself he was. Right away I remembered Jurek with that stick in the forest. I had no doubt: he would use the cane to whack people, like Mr Szujski had.

Sure enough, the next moment Jurek struck Drugi hard on the arm.

"Ow!" cried Drugi, cringing.

Shocked, for a moment we just stood there, unsure what to do. But the next moment Drugi, even though he was rubbing his arm, laughed.

His laughter released us. It was as if nothing had happened.

Except I was upset. Knowing that if Jurek won the cane, he would use it in the worst way – as he just had. And that told me that I absolutely couldn't let Jurek be the button king. He'd go crazy.

Jurek held up the cane. "The cane goes to the contest winner," he proclaimed. "And I'll keep it because that'll be me."

No one said or did anything. We all just looked at him. I had no idea what the others were thinking, but as I stood staring at Jurek, the only way I could figure out how to stop him was by winning the contest myself. When I did, the first thing I'd do was chop up that cane and burn the pieces.

26

That evening, when my friends and I gathered at the pump, it was Jurek who said, "Since the Germans knew when the Russians were leaving, they'll know when to get here."

"What's that mean?"

Jurek said, "First the bomb, then soldiers. Can't be an accident. Bet you anything, they'll come tomorrow. Someone is telling the Germans."

"Who?" said Drugi.

When no one said anything, Raclaw said, "Can't wait to see their buttons."

"Why?" Drugi asked.

"He thinks he can win the contest, stupid," said Makary.

I said, "I'm going to win,"

"Forget it," said Jurek. "I'll be the winner."

"Maybe," said Makary, and gave Jurek a shove.

"I'd like to win," said Drugi.

"You're too stupid," said Jurek.

We all laughed, including Drugi.

Raclaw said, "I just realized something: there are

no soldiers here. We can do anything. No laws."

"We should go to church and pray," said Ulryk.

"For what?" asked Wojtex.

"Us. The village."

"Waste of time," said Jurek. "Just wait for the Germans."

No one said a word, but I was sure we were all thinking about the same thing: buttons.

One by one, the others went off until Jurek and I remained.

"Going," I said, pushing off.

Jurek called after me, "Hey, Patryk! Accept it! I'm going to win. Whack!"

I wanted to snap out a smart remark, but I couldn't think of one. I didn't even look back. All I could think about was buttons. Not that I wanted them, just better ones than Jurek could get. I went home and told my parents about the bomb hole.

My father said, "People are saying the Germans will come tomorrow."

"How do they know?"

"Rumours."

"Do you believe them?"

"Rumours are like clouds. Sometimes they bring rain. Sometimes they don't. But there are always clouds."

"What do you think will happen?"

"We'll have to see."

"But," I said, "who are our enemies, the Russians or the Germans?"

All he said was, "Neither one are Polish."

I waited for him to say more. When he didn't, I went to bed.

27

It was the next day, in the late afternoon, with that hot August sun still beating down, when Jurek stuck his head through the door of my father's sweltering workshop and shouted, "The Germans are coming!"

I dropped the wheel work I'd been doing – smoothing spokes with a file – bolted out of the house and raced for the main street. By the time I arrived, it seemed as if the whole village had gathered again. People were standing about in small groups, talking, their voices tense and uneasy. But they kept turning from their conversations to watch the western road.

I took one look at the pump platform, saw that my friends had already climbed up, and joined them.

"Seen any Germans?" I asked.

"Don't worry – they're coming!"

"When?" said Drugi.

"Soon!" said Raclaw.

"With buttons!" said Jurek.

"Holding up their pants!" shouted Makary.

While they watched the road, I kept searching the sky. Though I saw nothing, I kept looking. From the corner of my eye, I noticed Jurek looking at me.

"What?" I said.

He mouthed the word *button* and pointed to himself.

Drugi said, "Hope they have buttons."

"Why?" I said.

"I'd like to·be king," Drugi responded with a shy smile.

"Not a chance," said Jurek.

Drugi's smile vanished. I thought he might cry.

The Germans announced their arrival with sudden and loud music. The abrupt blare caused a flock of birds to burst into flight, black spots against the sky. *Little aeroplanes*, I thought.

Villagers scurried to either side of the street. We

boys stayed on the platform, eager for a sighting. Jurek had climbed up on a pump wheel, determined to be the first one to see them.

The music drew nearer, more raucous, full of power. There was something stirring about it. It made us boys just about dance on the platform.

"I see them!" shouted Jurek from his perch.

The first of the Germans to appear were their drummers, pounding loud and insistent. Following them were soldiers playing shiny, blaring trumpets. Then came soldiers with bright and booming tubas.

Right behind the marching band came a flag bearer. He was holding up a large, flapping flag with a big black-and-white cross. In its middle was a single-headed eagle, its blood-red tongue sticking out like a flame.

There was another black cross in the upper left corner, the cross like the ones on the aeroplanes, on a black, white and red field. Officers came next, five of them, all on fine horses. The first officer, in the lead, was on a coal-black horse, which nodded its head and pranced with grace. To my eyes, it was all fine.

The captain's uniform was a tight-fitting tunic with a high collar and a double row of gold buttons down his chest. On his head, a cap with a visor. Black boots almost reached his knees. On his right side, hanging from the shiny leather, was a pistol in a holster. On his left, dangling from the same belt, was a sword. His tunic had an emblem, the same black cross that I had seen on the aeroplane.

Four other officers, looking much the same, followed their commander. Just behind were a few soldiers who had pale-blue uniforms.

Then the regular German soldiers arrived. At least a *hundred* of them – maybe more – marching in step, one with the other. Their trousers were dark green, their jackets the same colour, but bordered in red. All wore a brown helmet with a pointy spike on the top along with the number 136 in red. Each one had calf-high boots and a brown leather belt, to which leather pouches were attached. On every soldier's back was a rifle fitted with a bayonet.

Faces were stiff, eyes looking straight ahead. I didn't see one smile or frown, and their arms swung in perfect harmony. The firm *tramp-tramp* of their feet upon the street stones was sharp and precise. The whole troop moved like a single multilegged insect, fierce, so much more powerful looking than the Russians.

No wonder the Russians retreated! I thought, and

decided if I were to become a soldier, I'd be with the German army.

As powerful as the Germans appeared, what most interested me were the shiny-looking buttons running down each soldier's jacket.

"Do you think those buttons are silver?" said Raclaw.

"Don't worry," said Jurek. "I'll get one soon and tell you."

"Me too," said Drugi.

"This is the best dare ever," said Makary.

28

Just before the troops reached the pump, a mounted officer who had been behind the captain cantered forward, approached the pump platform, and made a waving motion with some kind of stick. It was clear he wanted us to get off. We leaped. The same officer got off his horse, climbed on the pump platform, and with arms on hips, feet spread wide, spoke in a loud, slow voice.

"Citizens!" the officer called out in Polish. "Is there one among you who can speak German?"

Raclaw's father came forward. He was wearing a black suit, white shirt and grey cravat. He had his hat in his hands.

"Name?" demanded the officer.

"Wozniak. I am the lawyer here."

"You will translate what the captain says."

The German captain spoke, and Raclaw's father – speaking in a loud voice – translated his words into Polish.

"The armed forces of Kaiser Friedrich Wilhelm have come here to liberate you from the tyrannical Russians. From this moment on, you are free."

The village people just listened.

"Do as you are told and we shall live in perfect harmony. Long live Kaiser Friedrich Wilhelm!

"Some of His Majesty's soldiers shall occupy the Russian barrack. The rest of them you shall welcome into your homes. Treat them well, and they shall treat you well.

"I congratulate you on your new freedom!" With that, the captain made a sharp salute and climbed down. He even shook Raclaw's father's hand.

There was no cheering from the village people.

Rather, they turned and moved away in sullen silence.

When the German captain and his officers marched off with the magistrate and Raclaw's father, the regular soldiers broke ranks and dispersed, many crowding into the tavern.

We boys went back to the pump platform.

First thing Jurek said was, "See all those buttons?"

"Lot of different ones," said Raclaw.

Once again, Drugi said, "How am I supposed to get one?"

Jurek said, "What do you think?"

"Won't they mind?" said Drugi.

"Just don't be dumb about it," said Makary, and he smacked Drugi on the head.

Wojtex said, "Remember Jurek's rule. You can't ask. You have to take."

Ulryk said, "But don't steal."

"Watch out for bayonets," said Jurek.

"I'm going home," I announced.

"Everyone!" Jurek yelled as we scattered. "Tonight. Midnight. Meet at the pump! Bring your new buttons!"

29

Makary walked with me. It was when we started off, and we chanced to look back, that we realized that following the German soldiers were large wagons pulled by horses. On the wagons were cannons. Two other wagons came by, mounted with some kind of smaller guns. We stopped and looked.

"Machine guns," said Makary.

"What's that mean?"

"I think they shoot very fast."

Those wagons were followed by other wagons that were full but covered with canvas.

"Full of ammunition," said Makary. "Lot of people going to get killed."

"Who?" I asked.

"Russians, I guess. You going to get buttons?" Makary asked me.

"Can't let Jurek be king. He'd be awful."

"I know," agreed Makary. "You saw: he'll use the cane to pound everyone. I'd like to win, but if I don't, I hope it's you."

"Why?"

"You won't beat on us."

I liked Makary for saying that. But it made me feel I absolutely had to do what he said.

30

When I got home, it was almost as if nothing had happened. My mother was in the kitchen, sewing. The soup in the iron pot was simmering. Made me feel hungry.

"Did you see the Germans?" I asked.

"Of course," she said. She put down the needle and rubbed her hands.

I stood there, waiting for her to say more. When she didn't, I said, "Do you think they will be bad?"

"We'll have to see."

I went into my father's workshop, where he was working, balancing a new wheel.

"They brought cannons," I said. "And machine guns."

My father sighed and shook his head.

"What are we going to do?" I asked.

"What we do is work," he said. Then he faced me. "Soldiers' work is to carry guns and use them. Stay out of their way."

"Russians have guns, too."

He held up both hands and shook one. "The Russians are here." He shook his other hand. "The Germans are here." He shook the other hand. "Who do you think is in the middle?"

"Us."

He brought his hands together with a loud *clap!* "It's dangerous. Make sure you understand."

"I do," I said.

My father and I worked. It was in the late afternoon that we heard a hard rapping coming from the front door.

"Dear God," my father murmured. He stood up, one hand pressed on his lower back.

He and I went into the front room. The door was open, and my mother was standing off to one side. A German soldier had already come into the house. He filled the small room, looming over my mother.

He was not a young man, and his spiked leather helmet made him appear very tall. In need of a shave, he had a tired, irritable appearance. What I noticed most were the eight bright buttons on his dark-green tunic, the tunic with red edging. In his hands was a rifle, a bayonet attached.

He said something in German, which didn't sound friendly. He looked at my mother, my father, and then at me, as if measuring us. There was no friendship in his gaze. He glanced at my parents' bed.

Holding the rifle in one hand, he pulled off his helmet and tossed it onto the bed, as if claiming it. Using his rifle as a kind of stick, he waved me and my parents away. He pointed towards the kitchen.

I looked at my parents for instruction.

"He wants us to leave him," my father said.

"Leave?" said my mother.

"He wants this room. To sleep."

"Dear God," my mother murmured, just as my father had said.

The soldier yelled and again pointed to the kitchen door.

My mother scurried out of the room first, followed by my father. They avoided looking at the German. I was the last to leave the room. As I went into the kitchen and shut the creaky door behind me, I glanced back. The soldier had begun to unfasten his tunic, one button at a time.

Elated, I thought, *I'll wait for the soldier to go to*

sleep. Once he does, I'll cut off at least one of those bright buttons.

My parents and I sat in the kitchen and ate our dinner of potatoes and cabbage soup along with bread. Aware that the German soldier was in the next room, we didn't talk much and when we did, we kept our voices low.

Whispering, I asked, "How long do you think he'll stay?"

My father's answer was, "Use the back door. Keep out of his way."

"I know," I said, and put on what I thought was a meek face. All the while, I was planning how I'd get one of the German's buttons.

31

That night, my parents went to sleep on the floor of the workshop, but I remained in the kitchen. I could hear my mother praying for longer than normal. I heard my father pray, too. He didn't do that very often.

I waited.

I searched about for my mother's kitchen knife. When I found it, I put it on her cutting board, in easy reach. I climbed up to my sleeping shelf, but having no intention of sleeping, kept my clothes on. I did make sure to take my good Russian button and put it in my box of special things.

I waited.

I have no idea what time it was when I crawled off my sleeping shelf. I might have even dozed. It didn't matter. Standing barefooted on the kitchen floor, I stayed still until my eyes became accustomed to the gloom. Everything was dark and silent. I listened, but heard nothing to alarm me.

Knowing I might need to get out fast, I made sure that the door that led from the kitchen to my father's workshop was closed but not locked.

Then I retrieved my mother's knife from where I had put it, gripped it in my right hand, and went towards the door of the front room. I pulled the door open a crack. It made its regular squeaky noise. I put my ear to the gap and listened.

At first, I heard nothing. The more I stayed there, however, the more certain I was that I could hear the German's sleeping breath, steady and slight.

I eased the door open a little further, enough to

stick my head into the room. Moonlight came through the window so that I could see the soldier in my parents' bed, the big feather-stuffed quilt pulled up to his stubbled chin. His arms and hands were under the quilt. His head, with his short, spiky hair, was propped on a pillow. His eyes were closed, mouth wide open, uneven teeth protruding. As I listened, his breathing sounded louder. I was sure he was asleep.

I glanced around. The German's boots were on the floor. So was his spiky helmet. As for his tunic, it hung from the bedpost at the foot of the bed. I could just see the row of buttons.

I opened the door a little more, enough for me to slip through. Once within the room, I stood without moving, waiting for my heart to calm down, all the while clutching the knife in my hand.

With a sudden grunt, the soldier shifted his body, turning to his right side.

My heart lurched.

The soldier was now facing me, eyes closed. A dab of spittle leaked from the corner of his mouth. If he had opened his eyes, he would have seen me standing there, three feet from where he lay, knife clutched in my hand. I was sure that if he woke, he would kill me.

I stood still, my heart pounding.

He continued to sleep.

I waited. *Do I really want to do this?* I asked myself. My answer: *Can't let Jurek win.*

I took two small steps closer to the bed.

The soldier didn't move.

I took another step. Once near the end of the bed, I sank to my knees. From there I reached out to the soldier's tunic, grasped a button with the fingers of my left hand, and pulled. With my right hand, I sawed behind the button with the knife, just as I had done at Jurek's house when getting the Russian button. It made a tiny rasping sound.

The button dropped so fast it slipped out of my fingers, hit the floor with a sharp *ping!*, and rolled under the bed.

32

I was afraid to breathe.

When the soldier didn't move, I bent over. I could just see the shining button under the bed.

I checked the soldier. He lay still.

Trying to make no noise, I stretched flat out on the floor, moved deep under the bed, then curled my fingers around the button. Even as I did, the soldier gave a muffled grunt and turned over. The bed creaked above my head.

Too fearful to move, I tried to think what I should do if the soldier woke and discovered me.

When the soldier's breath continued at a steady state, I slithered backward, out from under the bed. Afraid to stand, the knife in one hand, the button in the other, I crawled back to the kitchen door and butted it with my head so that it opened wider.

I slithered into the kitchen. Once there, I stood up and shut the door with care. Then I leaned against it and allowed myself some deep breathing. My heart was still pounding.

After putting my mother's knife back in its place, I shoved the new button deep into my trouser pocket – closing my fist around it. I didn't even bother with my boots but made my way through my father's workshop, careful not to step where my parents lay asleep on the floor.

No one woke.

I got outside through the back door. Full of excitement, gripping the button in my pocket, I ran.

33

Soon as I reached the main street, I took my fist from my pocket and, for the first time, tried to see what I'd stolen.

Less than an inch wide, the button was made from some kind of bright metal. For a moment, I thought it might be gold. Knowing that wasn't likely, I decided it was brass. Still, it was bright, which gave me lots of pleasure. I leaned against a building window, which, though its shutters were closed, cast out some light. When I drew the button close to my eyes and tried to make out its design, I saw two crossed cannons over three cannonballs.

Cannons! I was certain that none of my friends could have got anything better.

Excited, I stepped onto the main street and headed for the pump platform. Hearing a noise, I glanced up. Two German soldiers were in the middle of the street. They were standing next to each other, rifles on their backs, and they were looking right at me.

With a shot of panic, I shoved the button back into my pocket.

One of the soldiers beckoned me closer.

I did as he indicated and stood before the two soldiers. Feeling shaky, I had to force myself to look at them and did it with as innocent a face as I could muster.

They studied me in silence.

"What are you doing on the street at this hour?" one of them finally asked in Polish.

"I couldn't sleep, sir."

"Do you know what time it is?"

"No, sir."

"Midnight. Where are your parents?"

As I pointed back towards my alley, I could feel the button in my pocket. *If they search me and find it, I'll say I picked it up from the street.*

"Do they know you are out?"

"No, sir."

The other soldier asked, "Who do you like better, Russians or Germans?"

"Germans, sir," I said, thinking that the safest thing to say.

"Good. But do you know what might happen if you sneak around at night?"

"No, sir."

"We might think you were a spy," said the German.

"For the Russians. Do you know what would happen to you?"

"No, sir."

"Quick as anything, you'd get executed."

"Executed?"

"Shot."

"Yes, sir. I know, sir."

"Now, where were you going?"

"To the pump platform."

"Why?"

"When I can't sleep, I like to meet my friends there."

"We saw some boys there. Those your friends?"

"Think so."

"We spoke to them. Told them that if they worked harder during the day, they would sleep better at night." The soldier smiled down at me. "Now, get on with you. Stay out of trouble. You don't want to get yourself shot, do you?"

"Yes, sir, no, sir," I said. As I went off, I could hear the soldier speak to the other in German. There was laughter. I suppose he was sharing our conversation, how he thought he had scared me.

Pleased with myself, I ran on.

34

Jurek and Makary were sitting on the pump platform. They had stuck a lit candle on the concrete between them. As I approached, Jurek called, "Thought you'd scared out."

"Some German soldiers stopped me. Wanted to know what I was doing out at night."

"What did you tell them?"

"That I couldn't sleep."

"They came here, too," said Makary. "Asked us the same."

"What did you say?"

Jurek said, "That I sleepwalk."

"You didn't!"

"He did," said Makary, laughing.

Jurek said, "They warned us that if we wandered around at night, they might think we were Russian spies and shoot us."

"Told me that, too," I said.

"Stupid," said Jurek. "They aren't going to shoot a kid."

I looked around. "Where're the others?"

"No idea," said Jurek. "You get anything?"

"Did *you*?" I said.

"Asked you first," said Jurek.

"Yeah, I did."

"I got a good one," Makary put in.

"Let's see," said Jurek.

Makary put a button on the cement next to the candle. I peered at it. Jurek handed me his magnifying glass. Makary's button was bright like mine, though somewhat smaller. On it was a raised number ten.

I said, "What's that *ten* mean?"

Makary shrugged.

"Tenth Army," said Jurek as if he knew. "Or Tenth Regiment. Something like that."

After studying the button, I handed it back. "How'd you get it?" I asked.

"I went by the tavern. A German soldier was sitting there by the door, his back against the wall. Drunk. I sat right next to him and said, 'Can I have one of your buttons?' He mumbled something that I decided meant 'Yes'. So I just yanked it off his jacket. He didn't even notice."

Jurek said, "You're not supposed to ask."

"You can't make up all the rules," Makary shot back.

I looked at Jurek. He said, "The whole point is to do something brave to get one."

I said to him, "What did you get?"

Jurek held out the button. I took it and looked at it, then reached for the magnifying glass. In the dim light, it took a moment to make sense of what the design was.

"Is that a crown?" I asked.

Jurek nodded. "Bet it's the German king's crown."

I brought it up closer to my eyes, even as I stooped to get better light. Jurek was right: it was a crown. I liked it, but what went through my mind was, *My button is best.*

"What's it supposed to mean?" I asked.

Jurek said, "That the soldiers here are the German king's best soldiers. The finest in the whole German army. Right here. Because I'm here," he added.

I said, "How'd you get it?"

"A soldier came to our house. He spoke Polish, too. He told my sister to make him a meal. I could tell she liked him and when she served him, he sat down and took off his tunic. I offered to hang it up. When I did, it was easy. *Zip!* Button popped right off. What did you get?"

I pulled my button out of my pocket and held it

out. It was obvious that it was bigger and brighter than their buttons.

"Was it hard to grab?" asked Makary.

I told what I'd done.

Makary said, "Pretty good."

Jurek said nothing.

"Cannons," I said because it was obvious Jurek wasn't going to say anything. "With cannonballs," I added. "Better than a plain old number ten or a stupid crown."

"A crown is more important than cannons," said Jurek.

"Isn't," I said. "Anyway, my button is brighter. The contest is over."

The boys passed my button back and forth. I glanced at Jurek. I was sure he was jealous.

"Patryk's right," pronounced Makary. "A cannon is better than a crown."

"See?" I said to Jurek. "I win the contest."

"No, you don't," he said. "The contest is for everyone. We have to wait till the others show up with what they got."

"Where are they?"

"Don't know."

"I suppose..." I said, conceding. I held out my

107

hand and got my button back. I said, "I'm going home."

"Me too," said Makary.

I headed off. Behind me, Jurek shouted, "Patryk! I'm going to win!"

"Not if I can help it," I called back.

I continued towards home. As I did, I began to hear booming noises. I stopped and tried to figure out where they were coming from. The east. In the direction of the forest. As I continued to look that way, I saw bright flashes of light.

Something huge was happening.

35

Within moments, the street filled with German soldiers, most of them rushing from the village houses where they had been sleeping. They were in varying degrees of dress, some still putting on their jackets. Others buttoning them. Spiked helmets were on. All gripped rifles in their hands.

More soldiers appeared, probably from the

barracks. I ran back to the pump platform, climbed up, and looked east. All along the dark eastern horizon were flashes of light. The booming continued, too.

Jurek and Makary returned. They got up on the platform to see better.

"What do you think it is?" I asked.

Jurek, as usual, had an answer. "Russians. They're attacking."

"*Here?*" Makary's mouth hung open.

"Of course."

"But what's the noise?" I said.

"Cannons, stupid," said Jurek. He turned to me. "Not like the stupid ones on your button."

We watched the German soldiers gather in the street. Villagers appeared, too. It was dark, but I could see that everybody was facing east. The soldiers looked worried.

I turned to Makary. "Think they're scared?"

"Doubt it," Jurek answered for him.

Wojtex showed up. "My father wants to know what all that noise is."

"The Russians are attacking," said Jurek.

"*The village?*" cried Wojtex with alarm.

"Probably."

"I better tell my father," said Wojtex, and rushed away, arms pumping.

German officers began to appear. None of them were dishevelled. They started to shout orders. The German troops hastened to line up in marching order. From somewhere, other soldiers dragged out the wagons on which the machine guns had been mounted. I saw the soldier who had been in my house. I wondered if he realized a jacket button was missing. Nervous, I felt it in my pocket. To my relief, he never even glanced in my direction.

More orders were shouted. The soldiers began to march east towards the booming. There was no music.

"I better get home," Makary announced, and he hurried away.

Not sure what to do, I looked to Jurek.

Jurek said, "I'm going to see what they do." He leaped off the platform and began to run after the last of the Germans. After a few yards, he paused and looked back at me. "Come on!" he called.

"What if they think we're spies?" I shouted.

"Not a chance," he yelled, and kept running. As usual, he was daring me.

I wavered for a moment and then ran after him.

36

The quarter moon - low on the horizon - along with faint stars, provided only dim light, just enough to make our road glow like a white ribbon. To either side, farmland lay in darkness.

Jurek and I caught up with the tail end of the German troops. In the gloom, I thought the soldiers looked like marching ghosts, the steady *tramp* of their boots beating out the time. Beyond them, the light bursts continued, as did the booming. Each burst made me blink.

Thinking it was safer to whisper, I said, "Where do you think they're going?"

Jurek said, "To fight the Russians."

"A battle?"

"Maybe."

"Getting killed?"

"What do you think, idiot?"

I halted. "But..."

"Don't come if you're too jumpy," he said. There was mockery in his voice.

I stood still, listening to the constant booming

and watching the flashes of light. I was scared and knew I should go home. But I went forward, following Jurek.

"If there are bodies," Jurek said, "might be some great buttons. Best chance ever. For me, anyway. Told you I'd win."

Before I could reply, he began to run after the Germans. I watched him. I also heard my father's voice in my head saying, "Stay out of their way. Do you understand? It's dangerous."

But what I was also telling myself was, *If I let Jurek win, it would be what Makary said: awful.*

"Wait up!" I called as I ran after him.

37

We had to stop about two miles beyond the village. The German soldiers had gathered in a milling crowd, the officers clustered in their own group. They seemed to be debating something.

Before them the whole forest seemed to be on fire, with red-and-yellow flames reaching gigantic heights.

It roared, along with sounds of crackling, snapping, and what I thought were the thuds of crashing trees. Even from where we stood, behind the troops, I felt great heat. The air was thick with heavy smoke, making it hard to breathe. My eyes smarted. Sparks, like swarms of fiery insects, flew everywhere.

Jurek and I held back awhile, but with him leading the way, we stepped around the troops until we were alongside the foremost of them, facing the flaming forest. The Germans had reached the place where the aeroplane had made a crater in the road.

The soldiers paid us no mind. They were too intent on the inferno, their wide-eyed, apprehensive faces made ruddy by the light of the fire. A few had cigarettes dangling from their lips.

A shrill whistling sounded, followed by a flash of light, then a loud *whoomp!*

I jumped back, bumping into Jurek. He shoved me away. "Just a cannon shot," he said.

Putting my hand into my pocket, I squeezed the stolen button and thought of cannons and cannonballs. I said, "Why would the Russians set the forest on fire?"

"Know how we like to hide in the forest?"

I nodded.

"Same. They don't want Germans hiding there."

Jurek and I continued to stay where we were. There was more shelling, more explosions. A large scarlet chunk of wood dropped out of the sky and landed a few feet from where we were standing. Startled, we leaped away and watched it turn from rosy to grey ash, as if dying.

There was a shouting of German commands. As soon as they were given, the soldiers turned, formed into lines, and began to march back towards the village, rifles on shoulders. The machine-gun wagons followed. Within moments, almost all of the soldiers were gone. Four soldiers were left, plus Jurek and me. One of the remaining soldiers yelled and pointed, telling us to get away.

Relieved to be ordered to leave, I said, "We better go."

With a last look at the burning forest, Jurek and I headed back to the village. As I went, I felt the heat on my back.

We walked in silence, now and again turning to look at the burning. It wasn't only flashes we saw, but what seemed like a vast dome of trembling light where we knew the forest was. Or had been.

"That was an old forest," I said.

"Least a thousand years old. Belongs to me."

"Do you think it means the Russians are going to come back?"

"You sound like Drugi. But I'll answer you anyway: they *are* back."

Jurek had a way of making you feel like a fool. I shut my mouth.

38

When we got back to the village, burning torches on poles had been stuck up on the street to give light. The stench of burning was heavy, and layered smoke drifted through the air. From a distance, the booming continued.

There were lots of German soldiers on the main street. It looked as if they were just waiting to be told what to do. I saw the soldier who had been at our house sitting on the machine-gun wagon. He looked tired, and sad, as if he wanted to go back to bed. He paid no attention to me.

Jurek and I went to the pump platform. Makary

had come back. Ulryk, Raclaw and Wojtex were there, too. But not Drugi.

"Where you been?" called Raclaw.

We told them what we had seen.

"Is the whole forest gone?" asked Ulryk.

"Maybe," I said.

"Looks like it," said Jurek.

"What do you think the Germans will do?" Raclaw asked.

I shrugged. Feeling safe made it easy to act indifferent.

"What about the Russians?" said Wojtex.

"They'll attack," said Jurek with his usual authority.

"*Here?*" said Ulryk, alarmed.

"Sure."

Raclaw squirmed on his seat. "That's not so good."

For a while, no one moved or spoke but remained seated on the pump platform. We were facing east, listening to the booming, watching the light. The flashes flickered on the faces of my friends. Everyone was tense.

Jurek said, "Anyone get buttons?"

I said, "We should forget about buttons."

"Why?" asked Raclaw.

"It'll get us into trouble. The Germans might shoot us."

No one said anything until Makary said, "Here's what I got." He pulled out his button. It had the number ten on it.

Ulryk showed his button, which had a number six. We took turns peering at them.

Jurek said, "Ten beats six."

Makary said, "That's the first maths problem you've gotten right all year."

That broke the tension. We all laughed.

Raclaw held out his hand with his button. Jurek snatched it up and studied it. "Same as the one I got," he said. "The German's king's crown." He sounded disappointed.

Ulryk took the button and squinted at it. "It's got a crown with a cross on its top," he announced.

"Same as mine," said Ulryk.

"And mine," said Wojtex, showing it.

Makary asked Ulryk, "How'd you get it?"

Ulryk said, "There was a soldier staying at our house. I told him I was an altar boy at our church, and if he gave me a button, I'd pray for his soul. He gave me the button."

"That's asking," said Jurek. "Doesn't count."

Makary said, "You sound like you already won."

"I did," said Jurek. He showed his crown button.

Knowing I had the best button, I held it out so I could put an end to all this talk.

"Wow," said Raclaw. "Cannons. And bright. Might be gold."

The others crowded in to see it.

"Brass," said Jurek.

"It's the best," I said. "Contest over. I win." I lifted my hand. "I get the cane. Button king."

"No, you're not," Jurek said. "Drugi isn't here. Maybe he got a better one."

"Never," said Raclaw.

"Got to be fair," said Jurek. "We have to check."

I looked towards the east. "Now?"

Jurek said, "Have to settle the contest, don't we?"

I said, "It's too late."

"Fine," said Jurek. "In the morning."

"Sure," said Wojtex. "Morning."

I said, "Won't matter. I'm the winner."

We sat there and watched the forest fire glow and listened to more booming. One by one, we went off.

Far as I could tell, Jurek was the last to leave.

39

I got into my house through the back door. My parents were awake, sitting at the kitchen table.

"Where were you?" my father demanded.

"Just looking around," I said, and sat down. Nervous about speaking, I glanced towards the bedroom.

They understood my meaning. "He's gone," said my father. Then, as my mother served us, he said, "What have you seen?"

I said, "The whole forest is burning."

My mother put down her pot. "What do you mean?"

"The Russians did it with cannons."

"Did you see it?" my father asked.

I nodded.

My father said, "Were you in danger?"

I shook my head.

"But ... why did they do it?" my mother asked.

I gave Jurek's answer: "Probably don't want the Germans to hide there."

My father said, "I told you not to do stupid things."

"It was fine," I said, acting easy, but I was glad to be home.

My father reached out and grasped my arm. "Please," he said, "be careful."

I said, "Do you think the Russians will attack the village?"

My father said, "I don't know anything."

We finished eating and then my parents went into the workroom to sleep. I climbed onto my sleeping shelf and lay down. For a while, I listened to the booming. After a while, I reached into my box and put my cannon button into it. As the booming continued, I fell into uneasy sleep, thinking, *What if the Russians attack the village tonight?*

40

When I woke up in the morning, it was raining, a heavy rain that beat down on our roof the way that Russian had beat on his drum, a constant rattle. I listened but could hear no booming. When I looked down from my shelf, I saw my mother at the table, sewing. Her needle was moving fast, which happened when she was tense.

"Did the German soldier come back?" I whispered, pointing to the front room.

She shook her head.

"Think he will?"

One shoulder lifted. She said, "Don't go into the room."

I took out my German button, looked at it, squeezed it, put it back in the box, then sat up and listened to the steady beating of the rain. Now and again, it thundered, rolling thumps and crashes, with an occasional crack of lightning. It was a big storm, but I thought how much safer it sounded compared to what I'd seen and heard the night before.

For breakfast, I had a bowl of milk and some bread. I wanted to get out and meet my friends, but the hard rain continued. That meant no one would be at the pump. I thought about Drugi. If he didn't have a good button, I'd be the contest winner. I'd be done with it and wouldn't have to worry about Jurek winning.

With the rain continuing all day, I spent my time working with my father. The German soldier did not come back. It rained that night, too, and into the middle of the next day, when it stopped.

Once it ended, I asked, "Do I need to get water?"

"Your mother got some."

"Can I go?"

"Where?" my father asked.

"My friends."

He said, "Remember what I said: be careful."

"I will." I went out into the alley, which was deep in mud from the rain. There was no fresh after-rain smell in the air, just a stench of burning. Low clouds were churning grey. Was I seeing smoke? I hoped the day and a half of hard rain had put out the forest fires.

I headed for the pump, my feet splashing in puddles. The main street was crowded with German soldiers standing about, all wearing their spiked helmets, rifles on their backs. Other equipment hung on their belts. Pokey and prickly, they looked like an army of wet hedgehogs. They seemed restless, wanting something to happen.

Villagers were trying to avoid the soldiers, stepping around them or keeping to the fringes of the street.

Machine-gun carts and a couple of cannon wagons were sitting near the pump. The soldier who had stayed in our house was on a wagon. I stole a glance at him. He paid me no mind. In fact, as I walked among the soldiers, no one paid me any attention at all.

When I got to the pump platform, there was a short line of women, buckets in hand, waiting to get water. Turning the pump wheel were Raclaw and Ulryk. I climbed up. "Want some help?"

"Thanks," said Raclaw, and stepped aside. I worked the wheel for a while.

The line of women ended. By that time, Jurek, Wojtex and Makary had shown up. We took our usual places on the platform.

"Do you think the whole forest burned?" asked Makary.

Jurek said, "Sure. It was still burning when I saw it."

"When was that?"

"Before," said Jurek, not being very precise.

"Wish I'd seen it," said Wojtex. He sounded wistful.

Ulryk said, "What do you think the Germans are going to do?"

Raclaw nodded towards the magistrate's house, across the way. "The German officers are in there. Bet they're trying to decide."

Makary said, "Maybe they'll attack the Russians before the Russians attack them."

"Where?" said Jurek. "Can't be the forest. That's the whole point of what the Russians did."

"My father," said Wojtex, "is worried that the Russians will attack here."

"I'd like to see that," said Jurek.

That's when Ulryk said, "Father Stanislaw told me we might have to leave the village."

I said, "Why?"

"There'll be a lot of fighting."

"Just soldiers," said Jurek.

I said, "Anyone know where Drugi is?"

Jurek turned to me and said, "You think you've won the contest, don't you?"

I grinned and said, "Yeah."

Raclaw said, "Have to be fair. If we're going to decide, we need to see what Drugi got. Let's go."

As one, we leaped off the platform and, with me leading the way, ran through the muddy puddle-pocked town.

41

Drugi and his family lived in a small wooden house just south of the village, next to a field where they grew potatoes. The family consisted of him, his mother, father, and an older brother called Arek.

As we approached the house, we didn't talk. Though pleased with myself, I tried not to show it. Jurek was silent. I was sure he knew I had won the contest and wasn't happy.

When we reached Drugi's house, I was so eager to find out what he'd got that it was me who pounded on the door. When there was no answer, I pounded again.

The door opened a crack. We could see an eye peering out. When the door opened a bit, we realized it was Arek, Drugi's brother. He said, "What is it?"

I said, "Is Drugi home?"

"Why do you want him?"

"Need to talk to him."

Arek said, "He can't talk."

"What do you mean?" I asked.

"He's sick." Arek opened the door further. A

teenager, he was short and stocky, with a thin thread of a moustache. He had a big purple bruise on his cheek.

"What kind of sick?" Jurek called out.

Arek was silent for a while, as if deciding what to say. "Beat up sick," he said.

"*Beat up?*" cried Ulryk.

"We had a soldier staying here."

"A German?" asked Makary.

"Austrian."

"We had a German one," I said.

"You know Drugi," Arek went on. "Not too bright. He got a notion to steal a button from the soldier. From his cap. Don't ask me why. The soldier caught him at it and beat him. Badly. I tried to stop the soldier. But he had a gun. Couldn't."

Shocked, we boys eyed one another but didn't say anything. We just stood there.

It was Ulryk who asked, "Is … is he hurt bad?"

Arek nodded and touched his own bruise. "In the middle of the night – when all that cannon shooting began – the soldier rushed off. He hasn't come back. If he does, I'm going to kill him."

It was Jurek, after a moment, who said, "Can we see Drugi? Tell him we feel sorry. Maybe it'll make him feel better."

I looked at Jurek with disgust. I was sure he didn't mean what he said. He just wanted to know if Drugi had a button.

After a moment, Arek pulled the door open further, saying, "He'd like that."

We squeezed into the small house, stepping into the main room. As in my house, a big bed took up most of the space. In the bed was Drugi. He was a small kid. Now he looked tiny.

We crowded around the bed and stared down. It was ghastly. Drugi's face was swollen and covered with dark-purple bruises and cuts, which stood out because his skin was as pale as bread dough. His puffy eyes were closed. There was dry blood around one eye and his mouth. One arm was atop the blanket, the other underneath. The arm we could see had a cloth wrapped around it. The cloth was stained red.

Sitting in a chair right next to the bed was Drugi's mother. His father stood next to her. He looked at us and said, "Drugi's friends are welcome."

"Is he ... dying?" Ulryk asked the parents in a whisper.

Drugi's mother's lips moved but I didn't hear her words. She also made the sign of the cross over her chest.

Ulryk leaned over the bed. "Drugi?" he said. "Can you hear me?" He was trying to act like the priest.

Drugi made no response.

"Drugi?" called Ulryk, a little louder.

No answer.

Jurek turned to Drugi's brother. "Did he get the soldier's button he was after?"

"Why would you ask that?" asked Drugi's father.

"Just … was."

To Drugi's mother, Ulryk said, "Should I get Father Stanislaw?"

She nodded, and tears came down her cheeks even as she made another sign of the cross. Ulryk pushed his way through us to the door.

Though we didn't talk, the rest of us hovered about the bed for a few more moments. I could hear my friends' agitated breathing, but we avoided looking at one another. I didn't know what I felt more, sick or angry.

No one told us to go, but we murmured something and then left.

With a small click, the door closed behind us.

42

We stood outside Drugi's house, not talking. It didn't matter that the brother didn't know why Drugi did what he did. We knew.

Jurek said, "Drugi never was that smart."

"You don't have to be mean," I said.

"Yeah," said Makary. "I liked his questions."

"They were dumb," said Jurek.

"Then how come we never had answers?" said Raclaw.

"Beaten for a button," I said. "We should have protected him."

"Sure," said Jurek, "you against the soldier's gun."

I glared at him.

Makary said, "What's an Austrian soldier doing here, anyway?"

"Friends with the Germans," said Raclaw.

Wojtex said, "German and Austrian, they both speak German, right? What's the difference?"

"Think their buttons are different?" said Makary.

"Have to be," said Jurek.

After a moment, Raclaw said, "Guess Patryk won the contest."

"No, he didn't," said Jurek.

"How come?" said Wojtex.

Jurek said, "Because the contest was for all seven of us. With Drugi gone, it changes everything. We're six now."

"Drugi isn't gone," I said.

"Looks it."

"And maybe he did get a button," I said.

Jurek shook his head. "Not Drugi."

I was so upset, I shouted, "You don't know! The contest is over. Anyway, it's too risky. I won."

Jurek said, "Nope. Starts all over again. Rules. We have another day. Just us six."

"Not fair," I said.

Jurek said, "Does everyone agree with me?"

There were some mumbles from the others.

"Five against one," said Jurek to me. "Contest goes for another day. Just us six," he repeated.

I shook my head and said, "We should stop."

The other boys looked to Jurek, as if he should decide.

"See?" he said to me. "You didn't win." Then he added, "I'm going out to the forest. See what happened.

Bet the rain put out the fire. Anyone want to come?"

"I will," said Raclaw.

"Me too," said Makary.

"I need to go home," said Wojtex. "My father gets worried." He walked off.

Furious, feeling bested, I hung back.

"You coming, Patryk?" said Jurek, with his smile. He was taunting me.

I knew one thing: if you're beaten by Jurek, the worst thing you can do is show him that you care about being beaten.

"Yeah," I said. "I'll go."

43

When we got back to the main street, there were still a lot of German soldiers milling around.

"They're waiting," said Jurek.

"For what?" I said.

"To see if they're going after the Russians," said Jurek. "Or maybe they're waiting for the Russians to come after them."

"Think they will?" asked Raclaw.

Jurek said, "It's a war, isn't it?"

To Raclaw, I said, "See any Austrian soldiers?"

Raclaw looked about. "Over there," he said, pointing.

There were two of them, their uniforms pale blue. They were young faced, standing a bit aside from the German troops. Both soldiers had packs on their backs, plus leather pouches on their belts. In their hands were rifles. They weren't wearing spiked helmets but caps with black visors.

"No buttons," said Makary.

"Yes, there are," said Jurek. "On their caps."

Sure enough, when I looked again, I saw that their caps had three buttons on them. I had no idea why. I wondered if either of the Austrians was the one who had beat up Drugi.

"Why they here?" I asked, hating them.

"Told you," said Raclaw. "Friends of the Germans."

"Some friends," I said.

"We going to the forest?" asked Jurek. Impatient, he started off without glancing back, which made me wonder why he wanted to go so much. In fact, the others boys and I looked at one another – as if to make sure we were *all* going – but then we went along.

Telling myself that more than ever I had to protect my friends from this stupid button business, I thought, *I have to be smarter.*

But I went.

44

The day was already hot and hazy, the humidity thick, the smell of burn heavy in the air. We set out by crossing the old bridge. The rain had made the river water high, causing it to tumble and froth, as if doing somersaults. We moved along the road in an easterly direction. Jurek was in the lead, in a hurry for his own reasons.

The roadbed wasn't smooth but full of muddy wheel ruts. Footprints from heavy boots were everywhere, too. In the farm fields to either side of the road, no one was working.

From time to time, I looked up at the western sky, half expecting to see an aeroplane. That brought that *clatter-clatter* sound into my thoughts. *Don't listen to it,* I told myself. *Keep your eyes on*

Jurek. He's the dangerous one.

The further east we went, the stronger the smell of the fire. I began to realize that the haze in the air *was* smoke, with its sour, heavy stench.

Raclaw said, "What if there are Russians in the forest?"

"Nobody will hurt us," Jurek assured us. As if he knew.

"Hurt Drugi," I said.

"Drugi wasn't smart," Jurek said over his shoulder. "Deserved a swatting."

"You're not supposed to say bad things about the dead," said Makary.

"He isn't dead."

"Won't be long."

Raclaw said, "Wish death, get death."

We kept on until we came upon a huge hole in the road. Another place where a cannon shell had hit.

Raclaw studied it. "This isn't the one we saw the day before."

"Much nearer to the village," agreed Makary. He stared down the road. "Maybe the Russians are close. What if we see them?"

Jurek said, "Run."

We laughed, but it was jumpy laughter.

We stood around the hole for a while, looking into it as if it might tell us something. There was nothing except dirt, rocks, and a pool of muddy water at the bottom. Except for Jurek, I don't think any of us wanted to go further.

"Come on," said an impatient Jurek. "Do I have to make it a dare?"

We skirted the hole and kept going. "Why would the Russians send cannon shot here?" asked Makary.

Jurek said, "Maybe they thought the Germans were sitting around. Trying to hit them."

Raclaw said, "Wonder what it feels like to be hit by cannon shot."

Makary said "You wouldn't have time to feel."

I said, "Ever think what it feels like to be dead?"

No one answered.

For a while, Makary took the lead. When he came to another crater in the road, he had no choice but to look into it. When he did, he gasped, made a cross over his chest, and whispered, "Dear God..."

I saw two crows fly up.

At the bottom of the hole lay two soldiers, one in a light-blue Austrian uniform and the other in the dark green of Germany.

The two lay on their backs, mud-splattered heads

thrown back, their mouths open, necks twisted. Streaks of blood oozed across the filthy brown water in which they lay up to their chests. A hand, or at least a three-finger claw, stuck out of the muck as if trying to grasp something. A bare toe also poked up. One of the soldiers had his eyes open, but he couldn't be seeing anything because his eye sockets were empty. The crows had been pecking at them. The other soldier's face – the Austrian – was covered with dried blood. His cap was still on.

Raclaw turned around and threw up.

The rest of us stood in horror-stricken silence.

Jurek turned to me. "Remember the other night, when the Germans marched away? They left soldiers on guard." I could do no more than nod.

Makary said, "Think the Germans know what happened?" He looked back towards the village, as if wanting to be there. "I think we should tell them."

"Me too," I said.

Jurek said, "That cap is Austrian."

"So what?" said Raclaw.

"Has buttons on it, right?" said Jurek. "Anyone dare me to get one?"

"That's disgusting," I said.

Jurek grinned, started to climb into the hole, and

began to work his way down, slipping and sliding in the mud.

"Don't do it!" I shouted.

"Dare, wasn't it?" said Jurek as he continued down, working to avoid the water.

We stood and watched. I was jealous of Jurek's boldness.

When he got close enough to the dead Austrian, he leaned over, reached out, plucked the cap off the soldier's head, and then held it up in triumph. Then he grasped the cap with his left hand and with his right yanked hard on one of the buttons. I heard the thread snap.

"Got it!" Jurek cried, and tossed the cap away. Muddy water seeped into it until it sank.

Clutching his button in a fist, a grinning Jurek climbed out of the pit. I felt nauseous.

Raclaw wiped his mouth with the back of his hand and said, "Stealing something from a dead man is a sin."

"You sound like Ulryk."

"Too bad," said Raclaw, trying not to look into the hole. "Anyway, a hat is a stupid place for a button. Isn't really a button. Doesn't close anything."

"Let's go back," I said.

Jurek rubbed the button with his fingers to make it brighter and then brought it nearer to his eyes. "Best ever," he announced, and held it out for everyone to see.

The button was about the same size as the others we had collected. This one bore the image of a bird with one head and on the bird's head was a crown. Its wings were spread wide. So were its claws. Like the Russian button, one claw held some round thing. The other held a sword.

"Looks like a cane," said Jurek with a grin.

It *was* a fine button.

"I win," Jurek said.

"No, you don't," I objected, trying to think of some way to stop him. "You said it began all over again. Another day. A whole day. The rest of us still have a chance."

Jurek gestured to the dead soldiers. "Help yourself."

"You sank that hat," I said. "On purpose."

"Too bad," said Jurek. "I'm going to look at the forest." He put his new button into his pocket, skirted the hole, and started forward.

I called at him. "Not fair!"

"Fine for me," said Jurek.

Makary said, "I'm going." He followed Jurek. Then Raclaw went, too, leaving me alone. I stood there. *Should I go or not?* I asked myself. *Why does Jurek want to get into the forest? What if he does something that gets Makary and Raclaw in trouble?*

Making an effort to avoid looking down into the hole, I trailed along even as I told myself it was a mistake.

We didn't have very far to go before we reached the edge of the forest. Or what had been the forest. Everything was black and grey. And silent. Only a few trees were standing, and those that were had almost no branches. Charred, jagged stumps, like broken fingers, poked up everywhere. Scorched tree limbs lay scattered on soggy ground. There were heaps of ash along with muddy puddles and shattered rocks with sharp edges. Here and there were large holes from which wisps of smoke or steam rose up, giving the air a rancid smell. In a few places, glowing embers lay embedded in the earth, like half-buried and sullen eyes.

We stood and stared in disbelief.

"It's all gone," I whispered, as if being loud would be wrong.

"Not even a place to hide," said Raclaw.

"Not sure I want to go in there," said Makary. "What if Russians are hiding?"

"Where would they hide?" said Jurek. "We'd see them. Come on. It's safe."

"I don't think we should," I said.

Jurek said, "You never want to do anything. Always scared. Let's go to the ruins."

"Why?"

"It's my ancestor's place, isn't it?"

Makary rolled his eyes.

"How you going to find it?"

"Don't worry. I can. Come on."

Jurek started walking, and he did seem to know the way. After a moment, Makary and Raclaw followed. Wanting to prove Jurek wrong about me being scared, I went, too.

The ground was so muddy, I sank into the damp earth as deep as my ankles. When I pulled my feet out, it made a soft sucking sound. It somehow reminded me of the sound my mother made when she kissed my forehead.

We went on, no one speaking, just following Jurek. I kept looking around and up into the dull sky. I was not sure what I was looking for. Something living, maybe.

When there was a sudden crash, we halted and peered around.

"Tree crashing," said Makary. But you couldn't tell which tree had fallen because so many trees were down.

"Think *anyone* is here?" whispered Raclaw.

"Maybe," said Jurek. He kept looking around as if in search of someone.

"Wonder what happened to the animals and birds," I said.

"Ran away," said Jurek. "Means it's just us." He spread his arms wide. "I own the whole forest!" he yelled. The words hung in the air as if they had nowhere to go.

Makary said, "You can have it."

"It's already mine. Let's go!"

We went on.

A little further in, I noticed the burned carcass of a deer. It was bloated, black and stiff. Its charred legs were like chair legs. "Look at that," I said, pointing.

Raclaw peered at it and made the sign of the cross.

"Ulryk said animals have no souls," said Makary.

Raclaw shrugged. "Maybe they do."

"Hope so," I said.

We kept on, moving in single file, Jurek in the lead. "I see the ruins!" he cried and pointed. It was as if there was but one ruin. To me, everything was a ruin.

We stood in the midst of it. The green tinge on the stones was gone. They were black now. But the chimney was still standing.

"Weird," said Makary. "Everything else wrecked. But this part, which was already wrecked, is still here."

"Yeah," I said, "the one dead thing is still alive."

"Maybe a wood witch protects it," said Raclaw.

"Think?" said Makary.

Raclaw said, "I've read about them."

"Reading is school," said Jurek. "There's no more school. Throw away your glasses."

I looked around. I felt cold. "We could make a fire in the old chimney," I suggested.

Raclaw said, "How you going to light it?"

I said, "I've seen embers."

Glad to do something, we gathered branches from the ground, a lot of them already half burned. We piled them in the chimney's hearth.

I said, "I'm going to look for fire. Anyone coming?"

Raclaw went with me.

After we had walked some distance, I stopped. Keeping my voice low, I said, "You ever think Jurek is crazy?"

"Sometimes."

"He scares me. We shouldn't do whatever he says. It's the button business that got Drugi."

"I know."

"We need to quit."

Raclaw stopped and looked at me. "You haven't."

"Want to keep Jurek from winning."

"He would be bad."

I noticed a curl of smoke rising from the ground. "Over there."

Raclaw found a branch with a pointy end. Using it, he poked at the earth. Just under the dirt, he found a glowing piece of wood. Even as we uncovered it, it flamed.

"If Ulryk was here," said Raclaw, "he'd say we found Hell."

"Maybe we did," I said.

46

I searched around until I found a slab of charred wood. Using it as a shovel, I dug up the ember.

We carried the glowing bit back to the old chimney and dumped it onto the pile of branches, then put more wood bits atop the smouldering ember. Makary, on his knees, blew on it. A fire soon blazed. The four of us sat before the flame, knees drawn up, facing the warmth. It felt alive.

"Should have brought some food," said Jurek.

"Some of Wojtex's sausages," agreed Makary.

"He's a stupid, fat ox," said Jurek.

"Do you like anyone?" I asked.

Jurek laughed. "Me."

No one spoke until Makary said, "Hope Drugi is all right."

I said, "Ulryk went to get the priest."

We stayed silent, staring at the flames. The sole sound was the snap and crackle of the burning wood. I was feeling jumpy, again wishing I hadn't come.

An owl hooted. We looked up and around.

"Told you," said Raclaw. "The place is haunted."

"See the owl anywhere?" asked Jurek.

Makary shook his head.

I said, "If it hoots two more times, I'm going home." I hoped it would.

We waited. No more hoots. Jurek cupped his hands around his mouth and gave a good imitation.

We laughed. Uneasy laughter. Angry at myself for being weak, I wanted to leave more than ever. I said, "I think the owl is telling us to go."

Makary said, "Fire can't hurt them. They're magical."

"Magic isn't real," said Raclaw.

From time to time, I looked up at the grey sky and at the deadness around me. I kept telling myself to leave. I didn't.

Abruptly, Raclaw looked up, "People are coming."

We sprang to our feet. Next moment, we were surrounded by soldiers. All of them had rifles in their hands and the rifles were pointed at us.

47

They were Russian soldiers, maybe a dozen. Among them, I recognized Commandant Dmitrov. The Russians were in their tan uniforms except one man. His uniform was a darker brown, and he stood a little aside.

Dmitrov looked at us and then broke into a smile. "Ah, Master Jurek, I was wondering when you'd come."

Surprised, I turned to Jurek. He was grinning. It was obvious: the Russians had been expecting him.

"And you other boys," the commandant went on, "you're from the village, aren't you? Always on the pump, right?"

"Yes, sir," said Raclaw.

Dmitrov gave an order to his soldiers. They lowered their rifles.

I kept staring at Jurek. He was looking smug.

Dmitrov said, "I know why Jurek is here. But the rest, what brings you?"

"We wanted to see what happened to the forest," said Raclaw. He had his eyes on Jurek, trying, I think, to make sense of what was happening.

"Not much left, is there?" said the commandant. "We did a good job, don't you think? Now, then, to business." He faced Jurek. "Let's hear your report. Are the Germans still in the village?"

"Yes, sir."

"How many do you think there are?"

Jurek said, "A hundred, maybe. And some Austrians," he added.

"Austrians?" continued the commandant. "How many?"

"Just a few."

Dmitrov laughed. "As you can see, we have our friends, too." He indicated the soldier in brown who was standing somewhat apart. "That man is an Englishman. A captain in the English army. The English are our allies."

We considered the newcomer. He wore a cap with a visor. Beneath his brown jacket was a khaki shirt and dark tie. There were leather straps over his shoulder and around his waist. A brown holster with a pistol was attached. I noticed the bright buttons on his jacket and wondered why he wore a tie.

Dmitrov said, "He speaks a little Russian. No Polish. Do you know why he's here?"

"No, sir," said Makary.

"He wants to see how brave Russian soldiers are."

The commandant grew thoughtful, twisting his moustache ends with his thumb and forefinger, shaping them into points.

Once again, he addressed Jurek: "Do the Germans have machine guns? Cannons?"

"Yes, sir," said Jurek.

"How many?"

Jurek said, "Two wagons with machine guns. The same for cannons."

Dmitrov said, "Where are the German officers living?"

Jurek said, "In the magistrate's home."

The commandant eyed us four boys, as if trying to decide what to do. The other Russian soldiers, guns lowered, continued to surround us. Their faces showed no emotion. The Englishman kept his distance.

"Very well," said Dmitrov. "Master Jurek, I promised you a reward." He looked down at his tunic and yanked off a button. He handed it to Jurek.

Jurek, puffed up, smiled, as if he had done something very clever, and took it.

"Now," continued Dmitrov, "I'm going to let you go. But when you get back to the village, I need you to tell the German officers that you and your friends went into the forest and that you saw four Russian soldiers. Understand? Just *four*."

"Yes, sir," said Jurek.

"Four?" I said, knowing that there were more than that.

"Four," said Dmitrov. "No more. Can you do that?"

Makary said, "But you're—"

"Never mind what you see. That's what you're to say. Understand? All right, then. Get going. Make sure you tell them 'four poor Russians'."

"Yes, sir," said Jurek.

"If you don't tell them, I know who you are and where to find you. On the pump. The fountain of youth. Am I right?" He laughed. "It won't go well for you if you don't do as I've ordered. Have I made myself clear? Remember: *four* Russian soldiers."

"Yes, sir," said Jurek.

"Do you want us to put out our fire?" said Makary.

"Just go. Four. Do what I ordered."

48

Following our own footsteps, the four of us walked from the ruins. I looked back. The Russian soldiers were standing in front of the fire. The only one watching us was the English soldier. I glanced at Jurek. He paid no attention to me.

"You're a spy for the Russians," I said to him.

"They wanted information. I wanted buttons."

"You'll do anything to win, won't you?"

"Better than losing."

"When did you talk to them?"

"During the rain. Some people are afraid of getting wet." He looked at me when he said that. "I went out to the forest. It's mine, isn't it? I was hoping they would be there." He looked at the button Dmitrov had given him. Frowning, he stopped walking. "I've already got one of these," he said with disgust, and threw it away. "All that for nothing." I think we were all too troubled to look at him. We just kept going.

To Jurek, Makary asked, "Why did the commandant want us to say there were four soldiers when there are more?"

"He can't count," said Jurek.

"That's stupid," I said.

Jurek, his voice full of mockery, said, "You're the ones who are stupid. Can't you guess? Because if the Germans think there are just four Russians, they'll come and try to get them. Then the Russians will ambush them."

"Ambush?" said Makary.

"What else?" said Jurek. "That's what happens in war."

That shut us up and we trudged on, but slower than before. It was me who said, "I don't want to tell them."

"What about the commandant's warning?" said Raclaw. "You heard him. He knows us. If the Russians get back into the village, he might... We have to do what he said."

"Hey," said Jurek, "what do you care? It's nothing to do with us. If there's fighting, we could get more buttons. Isn't that what this is all about? Good buttons." He pulled out the Austrian button he had taken from the dead soldier and held it up. "Otherwise, I win."

"You know what?" I said. "You *are* crazy."

Jurek laughed. "I like being crazy."

"Why?" I said to him.

"So you'll never know what I'll do next."

"If you win the cane," I asked, "then what?"

"I'll be king," said Jurek. "Did you see that Englishman's pistol? I'd rather have that."

"What would you do with it?" asked Makary.

"Use it," said Jurek.

No one spoke until I said, "We have to end this stupid contest. Look what happened to Drugi."

"But maybe I'll win," said Makary.

"See?" said Jurek to me. "Makary's right. It's only stupid if you lose. Remember: four Russians. If we do this right, I bet the Russians will give us great buttons. Or maybe the Germans will."

I said, "Whose side – German, Russian – are you on?"

"Mine."

"We need to stop," I said, "before someone else gets hurt."

No one replied. We kept moving towards the village.

49

The village magistrate's house stood on the main street, just opposite the pump. The grandest building in the village, it was a three-storey brick house, painted white. Four stone steps led up to the wide main door, which was flanked by two large windows.

When we four – Jurek, Raclaw, Makary and I – came near it, there were two German soldiers standing on guard in front of the steps. Wearing their pointed helmets – with the number 136 in red on them – they held rifles across their chests.

We stopped some distance from them and just looked. I said, "This isn't a good idea."

"I could ask my father," suggested Raclaw.

"We gave our word, didn't we?" said Jurek. "You heard Dmitrov; if he comes back, we'll be in trouble."

"We're just kids," said Makary. "Maybe they won't listen to us." He sounded hopeful.

"I'll speak to them," said Jurek. "Cowards stay back." He started forward, and it was the same as always: we followed. When we came up to the soldiers, we stood there, all in a row: four boys, dirty faced, caps on, boots muddy, staring at the soldiers.

It was Jurek who said, "We have something to tell your officers."

"Yes? What is it?" responded one of the soldiers in Polish. "Go on."

Jurek looked first at us – as if to include us in what he was about to say – then he said, "We were just out in the forest and we saw some Russian soldiers. Four of them."

"What?" cried the soldier. "Where?"

Jurek pointed east. "Out there. In the forest."

"How far?"

"Two miles. Then a little more."

"How many?"

"Four," said Jurek.

The two soldiers exchanged uneasy looks. The one who spoke Polish translated into German for the other. Then to us he said, "You sure they were Russians?"

"Yes, sir," said Jurek. "And one of them was an Englishman."

"English!" cried the soldier. "Wait here," and he hurried inside the building. The other soldier remained.

"This is bad," said Raclaw, but whether he said it to himself or to me, I wasn't sure.

To Jurek I said, "Why'd you tell him about the Englishman?"

"Get them excited."

The German soldier reappeared. "Come along," he ordered, beckoning us forward. "Quickly."

In a low voice, Jurek said, "Here come more buttons."

50

The four of us – three of us nervous – stepped beyond the door and found ourselves in a large hall with a high ceiling. There was a desk, behind which a German officer was sitting, piles of paper before him. Behind him was a closed door. Across the room was another shut door. Portraits of old men dressed in uniforms with many medals on their chests were framed in gold and hung along the walls.

The officer at the desk looked up. He spoke in German.

The Polish-speaking soldier responded in German. I assumed he repeated what we had said.

The Polish-speaking soldier said to us, "Where were the Russians?"

"In the forest."

"What were you doing there?"

Right away Jurek said, "Just looking around."

"How far away were they?"

"Few miles," said Jurek. "There's a ruin there. That's where they were."

The soldier translated for his officer.

The officer studied us for a few moments as if trying to decide whether to believe us. I hoped he wouldn't.

He looked down and shifted some papers around on his desk. Next moment he got up and gave a command to the soldier. The officer went through the door and closed it behind him.

To us the soldier said, "You will remain here."

Wishing more than ever that I'd gone home, I made a move to leave, but the soldier who had been outside the door was now standing behind us and blocked the way. I couldn't move. Instead, along with the others, I waited, fidgeting. During that time, I gazed at the pictures on the wall, wondering who the old men were.

The officer reappeared and said something to the soldier. The soldier said to us, "Do any of you speak German?"

Raclaw raised his hand. "A little."

"Good," the soldier said in Polish. "You will guide us to where you saw those Russians."

"Me, sir?" said Raclaw. His mouth was open. His eyes big.

In Polish, Jurek said, "I'll do it."

"No, him," said the soldier, pointing to Raclaw. "That's an order. Now go outside and wait. Don't leave."

We went outside and stood below the steps. Two German soldiers came along to make sure we didn't leave.

As soon as we stepped outside, Wojtex came running over from the pump platform.

"Where have you been?" he called.

"In the forest," said Jurek.

"It's all wrecked," said Makary.

"But we saw Russians," said Jurek. "With Commandant Dmitrov."

"And now," said Raclaw, "the Germans told us we have to lead them back to where the Russians are." He was on the verge of tears.

"Why?" asked Wojtex.

Jurek said, "To fight and capture them."

Wojtex gaped at us. "You going?" he asked, disbelief in his voice.

No one answered until Raclaw said, "I don't want to, but they're making me."

Jurek held out his new button, the one he got from the dead soldier. "Look what I got. It's Austrian. Which means I'm winning."

Wojtex, ignoring the button, said, "What if the Russians fight back?"

"That's what soldiers are supposed to do," said Jurek. "You want to look at this or not?"

"Guess what?" said Wojtex. "Drugi died."

"He did?" I said. Too many things were happening. I was beginning to feel panicky.

The next moment, the German officer came out of the magistrate's house. He shouted to one of the soldiers but he pointed at us. Then he rushed back inside.

The soldier he had spoken to turned to us. "You will all stay!"

Wojtex said, "I don't want any more buttons. I'm going home. Anyone want this?" He held out his Russian button. When no one offered to take it, he turned around and started off.

"Halt!" shouted one of the two German soldiers. He pointed his rifle at Wojtex and beckoned him to approach.

"But…"

The soldier strode forward, grabbed hold of Wojtex's arm, and yanked him back to where we were standing. As Wojtex was pulled, the Russian button he had been holding fell from his hand.

The soldier saw it, snatched it up, and examined it. Speaking German, he began to shout at Wojtex, who looked back with bewilderment.

Raclaw said, "He wants to know where you got it."

Wojtex, looking very scared, said, "I … I found it."

Before Raclaw could translate, the German soldier gripped Wojtex by the arm and started to pull him into the building.

"Get my father!" screamed Wojtex. "Get my father!"

The door slammed behind him. It all happened so fast we could do nothing but look at the closed door.

"What are they going to do with him?" whispered Makary.

"He'll be all right," Jurek said.

I said, "We have to stop this button business."

"We can't leave Wojtex," said Makary.

Next moment, twenty German soldiers came running up to the magistrate's house. They had their helmets on and were carrying rifles. Among them was that Polish-speaking soldier.

The officer to whom we had spoken burst out of the house, a pistol in his hand. He used his pistol to point at Raclaw, then pointed eastward. His meaning was obvious: lead the way.

"What about Wojtex?" I said. No one paid attention to me.

51

We headed down the street, staying close together, Jurek, Makary, Raclaw and I, though Jurek was a little in front as if he wanted to lead the way.

I looked back over my shoulder and once more said, "What about Wojtex?"

No one answered. I think they were all too caught up in what was happening. I kept looking back. The German soldiers had formed themselves into a double line and were marching some ten yards behind us. They were led by their officer, who gripped his pistol in his hand.

Raclaw, in a low voice, stammering, said to Jurek,

"Do you … do you really think it's going to be an … ambush?"

"Of course."

"But … but we're in front."

Jurek said, "If something starts to happen, just run to the side. Hide."

"But…"

"You want better buttons, don't you?"

"This has nothing to do with buttons!" cried Raclaw, who was getting more and more upset. "You're the one who cares about them! No one else does!"

"Shut up," said Jurek.

The German officer turned, shouted at us, and put fingers over his mouth, signalling to us to be quiet.

With no one speaking, we continued along the road. It appeared deserted.

Scared of a possible attack, I didn't know where to look other than ahead.

We passed the two cannon holes. We didn't stop but walked around them. The German soldiers didn't stop, either. They just split their ranks and marched around.

It was when we came to the third hole that we halted and looked down. It was impossible not to. The dead soldiers were still there. A swarm of flies, hundreds of them, crawled on the soldier's bloody face. It looked like a quivering mask. Their buzzing was loud enough to hear above the hole.

We boys looked back at the advancing Germans and waited.

The officer, drawing close, barked something.

Raclaw gestured to the hole. The officer peered down. After a moment, he turned to the soldier who spoke Polish and said something. The soldier translated: "When you came along here before and saw the Russians, were these bodies here?"

We nodded.

"How far is it now to where you saw the Russians?"

"In the forest," said Jurek. He pointed. "About a mile."

"Please, sir…" said Raclaw. He was squeezing one hand with the other until his fingers were white.

"Yes?"

"When we saw the Russians, we knew the commandant. His name is Dmitrov. He used to live in our village. Before you came. When he saw us, he said … he said we had to tell you there were four of them."

"And?"

"But, sir … there were … there were … more of them. And an English soldier."

The soldier translated for his officer. The officer's face paled. He snapped something to his soldier. To us the soldier said, "Then you lied."

"Please, sir," said Raclaw, cringing, "he said he'd punish us if we didn't."

That, too, was translated to the officer. Without warning, the officer stepped forward and struck Raclaw across the face. His glasses went flying, as did his cap. I leaped back in fright. The force of the blow made Raclaw fall to the ground.

The officer stood over Raclaw, grabbed his shirt, and yanked him up to his feet. Raclaw's cheek was marked by a red welt. He was crying.

Through his translator, the officer barked, "How many Russians? The truth now."

"T … twelve," Raclaw stammered. I felt as if my stomach was full of crawling worms.

"And … and an Englishman."

"Just one?"

Raclaw nodded.

"No more than a dozen Russians? Yes? No?"

"Yes," said Raclaw, sobbing. He tried to smear his tears away, but only managed to streak his face. Not knowing what to do, we stood still, staring. Makary, who was close to me, was trembling.

The soldier told the officer what Raclaw had said.

The German officer looked over his own men, as if counting.

He spoke to his soldier. To Raclaw the soldier said, "You will stay in front of us and lead us to where you saw the Russians. Absolutely no talk. None!"

The officer gave Raclaw a hard shove forward.

Stumbling, blubbering, Raclaw went past the hole with the dead soldiers.

I looked on the ground for his glasses but couldn't find them. I did see his cap and picked it up.

The soldier turned to me, Jurek and Makary. He made a waving motion with his hand. "Go home!" he said in Polish. "Go."

52

We scooted to the edge of the road.

The officer – his voice low – gave orders to his soldiers. They broke up their lines and spread out, three feet between them. Rifles in hand, they walked towards the forest, moving in crouched positions, as if ready to duck. The officer had his pistol in his hand.

Jurek, Makary and I stayed back and watched. Though the Germans were led by their officer, Raclaw was in front of them all. The officer kept smacking Raclaw's shoulder hard – I could hear the smacks – forcing him forward. Raclaw, head down, was sobbing.

"I want to see what happened to Wojtex," Makary announced, and he began to run back in the direction of the village.

"Anybody else a coward?" said Jurek, looking right at me.

Wishing I had gone with Makary, I watched him hurry down the road. Then I looked at Raclaw's cap, which I was still holding. I couldn't leave him. I stayed. But I didn't look at Jurek. Instead, the two of us watched the Germans edge into what had been the forest. I could no longer see Raclaw.

I said, "What's going to happen to Raclaw?"

"Don't know," said Jurek, "but I want to see." He ran down the road after the Germans. I followed, my stomach churning with fear.

When we reached what had been the forest

Jurek and I stopped. It was hard to see the Germans. They were spread out, rifles in hands, creeping forward among the burned-over trees.

I said, "I'm not going any further."

Jurek went on for a few more yards, then he too halted.

We stood and watched. I saw nothing of Raclaw, but I was still holding his cap, squeezing it. All I heard was my pounding heart.

There was a sudden burst of loud, rapid gunshots – *bang, bang, bang* – followed by what seemed like a hundred more bangs. Gunshots. The shots echoed and re-echoed then stopped.

The silence was terrifying.

and stared into the forest.

ed?" I whispered.

owder drifted over us. It had an

"Some kind of fight," said Jurek, his eyes big. For once I thought he was frightened.

"What about ... Raclaw?" I whispered.

"They're coming!" Jurek cried. "Run!" He raced off the road into a farm field. Not seeing what Jurek had seen but reacting, I ran with him. In seconds, we were in the middle of a field of tall rye. Once there, we flung ourselves down and lay as flat as possible, my face pressed hard against wet ground. My heart was thumping so hard it hurt. I found it difficult to breathe. Within moments, I heard the sound of fast running feet, lots of them.

I didn't dare move. Instead, I waited until everything became silent again.

Jurek said, "Stay down. I'm going to look."

"Be careful!"

He rolled over so that he was on his knees but still low. Cautiously, he parted the tall rye with his hands – as if opening a curtain – and peeked out.

"Nothing," he said.

Next moment, he stood up. "The Germans are racing down the road towards the village," he told me. "Just six of them and they're carrying a soldier."

"What about Raclaw?"

"Don't see him."

I stood in time to watch the last of the Germans rushing towards the village. Then I shifted to look at the forest, but couldn't believe what I was seeing: Russian soldiers – maybe two hundred of them, rifles in hands – were racing down the road in pursuit of the Germans. Commandant Dmitrov, in the lead, had a pistol.

"Get down!" I cried, and dropped.

Jurek did, too. "What was it?" he whispered.

"Russians! Hundreds of them. Going after the Germans."

"I told you," he said. "Ambush."

We listened as the sound of pursuing soldiers – like a herd of galloping horses – went past.

I was afraid to move.

It became silent again. We waited a while, then Jurek and I stood up, but slowly. When we looked down the road, there was no sign of soldiers, neither Russian nor German.

I said, "Where do you think they're going?"

"After the Germans. They'll try to take back the village."

"Was that really … an ambush?"

"Sure."

I said, "We … we let it happen."

"Nothing to do with us," said Jurek. "They made us."

I shook my head. "Buttons," I said.

Jurek shrugged.

We walked out of the field onto the road and looked towards the village. I saw no one. But from that direction, I began to hear more gunshots. Then there was an explosion. A column of black smoke rose into the air.

"What ... what do you think they did?"

Jurek said, "I'm going to find out." He took a few steps, stopped, and turned. "You coming?"

"What about Raclaw? He might need us. Be hurt."

"He can take care of himself," said Jurek, and he started, only to stop. "Coming?" he yelled.

"I need to find Raclaw."

"He'll be fine!" cried Jurek, and he began to run towards our village.

I watched him race down the road, then I turned and looked the other way, towards the forest. I didn't want to be alone, but I didn't want to leave Raclaw.

My hands mashed his cap.

I shifted around and began to walk towards the forest, first fast then slow, slower, then I stopped. I glanced back over my shoulder. I could no longer see Jurek. I started up again, towards the forest. I was shaking. I could almost hear my father saying I needed to help the weak.

"I don't want to be strong," I yelled to no one. I looked back to the village one more time, then continued to walk towards the forest.

A lot of soldiers had gone by. The earth was mucky, churned by boot prints. The forest appeared the same as before: burnt out, bare. The only colours were different shades of greys and blacks. The air smelled of rot. Silence was total. Nothing appeared alive. It was as if the whole world had died.

As I stood there, clutching Raclaw's cap in both hands, I realized I had no idea where to find him, or even if I could. *What if he's hiding? What if the Germans took him back to the village and we just didn't notice? What if he's been shot? Or wounded? What if he's dead...?*

I could think of only one place to try: the ruins.

Guessing which way to go, all the while looking around me, the word *ambush* continually poking into my thoughts, I walked with care, following those footprints. I came upon the body of a German soldier. He was lying face down in ashy muck. I gasped, stopped, and made the sign of the cross over my heart.

At first I was so fearful I couldn't do anything but stare at him. It took me a few moments before I moved forward and stood right over the body. That's when I saw a bullet hole in his back, from which a tiny ooze of blood had flowed. Still wet, it glistened.

I squatted down. "Sir?" I whispered, though it felt stupid to say such an ordinary thing.

When there was no reaction, I leaned forward, took hold of his jacket sleeve, and gave it a tug. When he still didn't move, I shook harder.

No response.

I let go a puff of breath, unaware I was holding it back. All the time, I was staring at the dead soldier, trying to make sense of it. *Who was he?* His uniform told me he was a German, but that's all. Then – it was the pistol in his hand – I realized it was that officer, the one who had struck Raclaw.

All I could think was: *He was alive a short time ago. I hated him. Now he's dead. And I feel sorry.*

I didn't understand my own feelings.

I gazed around as if there might be some answer visible. I saw two more German soldiers on the ground. They too looked to be dead. It was as if I was in a cemetery, the bodies not yet buried. I found it hard to breathe.

I made the sign of the cross over the dead officer, doing it the way I saw Father Stanislaw make the motion over Cyril at his funeral. I did the same for the two other dead soldiers.

I stood up. Though I wanted to go home, I looked for the ruins. All the while I was thinking, *What if I find more bodies? What if there are soldiers hiding? What if they – whoever they are – shoot me? How much further should I go? Where is Raclaw?*

"Raclaw!" I shouted. "Raclaw!"

There wasn't even an echo.

I forced myself to keep walking. It was as if I was falling deeper into the silence.

To my relief, I finally spotted the chimney ruin, although I had to stop and stare to make sure I was seeing it, that it wasn't another shattered tree. I edged forward, my breath rapid. When I reached the first of the old walls, I stopped and gazed about.

In the middle of the area lay another soldier's

body. He was all twisted, like a cloth doll that had been tossed away. He was on his back, face up, brown jacket in tatters, skin exposed, torn and bloody. I stared at him but didn't feel much emotion. I was getting used to the dead.

It took some gazing before I realized the man was the English soldier, the one who had been with the Russians, who was there to see how brave they were. It wasn't just his brown uniform: he was still wearing his necktie. *Why,* I wondered, *would he ever wear such a thing?*

Under him, just visible, I noticed the butt of his pistol, which he had carried. I also saw that dangling by a thread from his torn jacket was a small, golden button. In all that gloominess, it was like a bead of sunlight.

Leave it alone, I told myself.

But it might be a good one, I thought the next moment. *The only English one. Get it and the contest will absolutely be over. No way I couldn't beat Jurek.*

Though my thoughts made me uncomfortable, I moved towards the body, hesitated, bent down, and plucked at the button. It fell into my hand like a ripe berry. I looked at it closely. It was a fine one, polished and new, the image of an old-time cannon – on wheels – clear as

anything. I thought, *My father would like the wheels.*
Over the cannon was a crown.

Then, out of the corner of my eye, I saw Raclaw.

My heart gave a jolt.

He was sitting on the ground, back propped against one of the old stone walls. Not moving, eyes closed, his arms were by his side, palms up. The welt that had been made when he was struck by that German officer was distinct on his pale face, like a red scar.

My first thought was, *He's dead.*

Terribly frightened, I made myself draw closer.

"Raclaw...?" I whispered.

To my enormous relief, his eyelids quivered and then opened. He gazed at me with dazed eyes.

"It's me," I said, my voice ragged. "Patryk."

When he made no response, I said, "Do you know who I am?"

"P ... Patryk."

"Were … were you shot?"

He made a slight gesture with his right hand towards his left arm. It was enough for me to notice the blood stain on his sleeve.

"Got your cap," I said. I held it before his face. He didn't react, but I plopped it on his head, where it sat crookedly.

"Do … you have water?" he said in a small voice.

I shook my head. "What … happened?" I asked.

"What Jurek said. A … ambush with … with Russian soldiers. Lots of them."

"Did the Russians shoot you?"

He gave a small nod, closed his eyes – as if to keep them open was tiring – then said, "I didn't think anyone … would come. Do you have my … glasses?"

"I couldn't find them. What happened to that English soldier?"

Raclaw didn't seem to know who I was talking about.

"Can you walk back home?" I asked.

"Not sure."

"I'll help you."

"I can't see well."

Trying to think what to do and unable to know who I should be more afraid of, Russians or Germans,

I looked around. *What if we're attacked?* I thought. *What'll I do?*

I glanced at the body of the English soldier, and then back to Raclaw. His eyes were still closed. I went back to the Englishman's side and pried the pistol out from under his body, telling myself that I could at least try to defend us if we were attacked. Not that I knew if the pistol had bullets in it or even if it did, how to use the thing. All I knew was that you pulled the trigger.

Stuffing the gun into my trouser pocket, I turned back to Raclaw, hoping he hadn't noticed what I had done. I got down on my knees and adjusted Raclaw's cap so it sat better. Then I put my arm around his waist and struggled to get up, pulling him with me.

He gave a small moan, opened his eyes, and rose until he was standing unsteadily on his feet. Breathing hard, he leaned against me. For a few moments, we stood together, he resting, me trying to keep him from flopping down.

I said, "The Russians chased the Germans away. But I think there was fighting in the village. And that English soldier... He was killed. But ... I got a button. A cannon on wheels. And there's a crown over the cannon."

He didn't seem to care. All the same, I said, "I'm

putting it in your pocket. That way you'll win the contest."

"Just … want to get home."

"We're going," I said. "Tell me when you need to stop. Come on."

It took a long time to get out of the forest. We would walk awhile before Raclaw said, "Stop." I'd stop. He would breathe hard and then after a while he'd say, "All right." When we passed those dead soldiers, I don't think Raclaw even noticed.

Upon reaching the road, it was the same: we'd go for a while until he said he was tired. We'd pause. He would stand still, head bowed, eyes closed, taking deep, slow breaths. I kept watching the road, fearful that soldiers would appear.

"How far is it?" he asked any number of times.

My answer was always the same: "Close."

At one point he stopped and said, "It was my father…"

"What about him?"

"He sent a message … to the Germans."

"About what?"

"He told them when the Russians … were going."

"Why?"

"Hates Russians. That's … why the German … aeroplane came."

Shocked, I didn't know what to say.

We kept on, not talking. As we walked, I was aware of the English pistol bumping against my leg. Afraid to look at it, I was sorry I'd taken it but wasn't sure what to do. I kept telling myself to throw it away, but I didn't want Raclaw to see it. Though the road was empty, I was also scared that someone would appear and see it in my hand. I dreaded that they – whoever *they* were – would think I was a soldier and shoot me.

The pistol stayed in my pocket.

Not that it mattered. In all the time we walked along the road towards the village, we met no one. Nor was anyone working in any of the fields we passed. The burn stench stayed in the air. But the skies were blue and birds were flying.

About a mile from the village, I saw some soldiers on the road. There were four of them, all with rifles. Russians. Soon as I saw them, I halted. I wanted to throw the pistol away, but they were now looking right at us. I had to keep it.

We went forward. When we drew close to the soldiers, we stopped.

"You boys!" cried one of the soldiers. "What are you doing here?" He spoke in Russian.

I said, "We live in the village. My friend got shot."

"How did it happen?"

"I don't know. I just found him."

The soldiers looked at one another, as if trying to decide what to do. Then one of them made a gesture. "Come along," he said. "But from now on, you'll need permission to go in and out of the village."

"Yes, sir."

We went on. It was late afternoon. As we walked, I began to wonder what we would find in the village.

57

It was at the village's eastern edge that I first saw signs of fighting and destruction. Windows shattered. Doors broken. Holes in some buildings. Two buildings had been tumbled and looked like huge squashed bird nests. Villagers, faces filthy, eyes full of grief, were deep among the wreckage, pawing through splintered wood. But they hesitated, as if afraid of what would be found.

I saw no German soldiers but many Russian ones. I also saw some soldiers wearing uniforms I hadn't seen before: blue jackets and red trousers. I had no idea who or what they were. Village people were avoiding these military men, moving with caution, casting apprehensive glances at the soldiers.

The Russians were armed, but none seemed worried or ready to fight. Many were sitting on the ground, as if resting. Others were in small groups, standing around, talking among themselves. Smoking cigarettes. They paid no attention to us. Or anyone else for that matter. The fighting, for the moment, seemed to be over.

We passed a house, which had a wagon in front of it, a horse in its traces. People were loading furniture into it. It was obvious; they were leaving.

I wondered if my family would leave. Had anything bad happened to them? *Where*, I wondered, *would we – could we – go?* I had the thought: *I know nothing of the far world.*

We came to the River, and the bridge. Except there was no bridge. It had become shattered wood and lay in a tangled mound in the riverbed. Water – still high from the rain— rushed over the pieces. Even as I looked, some were pulled away.

On both riverbanks were stumpy, jagged posts, which had held up the bridge. Villagers were standing on both sides doing nothing more than staring, as if not believing what they didn't see.

With Raclaw leaning against me, I said, "The bridge is gone." I'm not sure Raclaw understood.

"What happened?" I asked a woman who was near us, Mrs Wukulski. A baker, she was a large woman, with big arms and a puffy face that looked like a round loaf of bread.

"When the Germans left," she said, "chased by the Russians – fast as they went – they blew it up."

"But ... why?"

She shrugged. "Slow down the Russians."

"Where did the Germans go?"

"West," she said, with a wave of her dimpled hand.

Raclaw whispered, "I want to get home."

Mrs Wukulski looked down at him as if just noticing. "Is that Raclaw? The lawyer's boy?"

I nodded.

"What happened?"

"Got shot."

"By whom?"

"Russians. I'm trying to get him home."

My face must have shown bafflement because Mrs Wukulski said, "I have to go that way. I'll carry him across."

I turned to Raclaw. Unsteady on his feet, he seemed to be looking at the riverbed, but I had no idea what he saw. I said, "Mrs Wukulski is going to pick you up and carry you."

Raclaw gave a small nod.

The woman bent over, scooped Raclaw up in her big arms, and held him across her chest. Moving sideways, she all but slid down the riverbank, bracing one foot against the steep incline. I followed.

She reached the rushing water and kept going. Water curled white against her long dress and legs. I came close behind, the water's chill making me shiver.

We walked across slowly. Mrs Wukulski felt her way with her feet, adjusting to the strong pressure of the water's flow. Every now and again, she paused to brace herself.

Raclaw, arms dangling, tried to keep his head up.

The water reached my waist. The current was powerful, and it was slippery underfoot.

Once on the far side, Mrs Wukulski, with Raclaw in her arms, struggled to climb the steep, slippery slope. At one point, she seemed about to fall backward. I came up fast and helped by pushing her from behind.

We got to the top of the bank, and though Raclaw was dry, Mrs Wukulski and I were dripping wet.

"Where's Patryk?" called Raclaw.

"I'm here."

Mrs Wukulski said, "Do you want me to carry you home?"

Raclaw said, "I can walk."

"I'll go with him," I said.

Mrs Wukulski set Raclaw down on his feet.

"Thank you," I said.

With Raclaw clinging to my arm, we moved towards his house. We had to make our way through bunches of Russian soldiers. They paid us no mind.

I saw a German machine-gun wagon that had been flipped over, the gun broken. I also saw two bodies on the ground. They looked to be dead but were so covered with mud that I wasn't sure which army they belonged to. Then I realized one of them was a kid. He lay face down in the mud, so I had no idea who he was. No one paid him any attention. I was afraid to stop.

Raclaw lived in one of the village's better houses on the main street, a two-storey brick building painted white. When we reached it, I could see that a window was shattered. I also saw holes in the wall, which, I realized, were bullet holes. The bullets had chipped away the white paint and exposed red brick, like a wound.

On his own – because he wanted to – Raclaw climbed the two stone steps – one at a time – that led to the wide door. He tried the door, but it wouldn't open. After taking a deep breath, he banged on it. His mother opened the door.

"Raclaw!" she cried, then enveloped him in her arms and pulled him into the house.

Next moment, the door slammed shut.

58

Exhausted, I stood outside Raclaw's house. For a moment, I thought of knocking on the door again and asking for that button I gave Raclaw. But I was uncomfortable with doing that. Anyway, I needed to go home and see my parents.

As I turned around, some armed Russian soldiers went by. It was then that I remembered the pistol in my trouser pocket. It felt bulky, obvious and unsafe. I wanted, needed, to get rid of it.

I stole a glance towards the pump platform, relieved not to see any of my friends. I didn't want them to know about the pistol.

Deciding what to do with it, I headed for home.

When I reached home, it seemed untouched. Even so, I hesitated about going in through the front door. I had no doubt that the German soldier was gone, but what if a Russian had come to replace him?

I went around the back and stepped into my father's workshop. He wasn't there. Nor was my mother in the kitchen. I stood there, speculating where they could be. Should I look for them? Stay home? In the end,

I decided to wait. Even so, to worry about my parents was something new.

I climbed my ladder to my sleeping place. Once there, I opened my wooden box and pulled the pistol from my pocket. It felt heavy and was wet from the river crossing, which made me wonder if it would still work. I didn't care. Just wanting to get rid of it, I put it in my box. Then I closed the lid, sure that my parents – or anyone else – would never look into it.

Weary, I felt I had to wait for my parents to return. I lay back on my sleeping shelf and thought about all that had happened. The ambush in the forest. Raclaw. The walk back. The village houses that had been destroyed. It was as confusing as it was horrible. I understood so little of it. Then into my head came the *clatter-clatter*, the aeroplane sound.

"Please go away," I whispered.

I thought about the button contest. As far as I was concerned, the English button had to be the best. Raclaw had it. That meant the contest was done. Which meant Jurek would not get to keep the cane.

My worry eased.

Though I tried to stay awake to see my parents, I was so tired, I fell asleep.

59

I slept through the night, woke, sat up, and looked down into the kitchen. The light told me it was morning. My mother was at the table, cutting up potatoes, putting pieces into her ever-cooking pot. She heard me stir, stopped her work, and looked up.

"We were worried. Where were you yesterday?"

"With my friends."

"Where?"

"Just around."

"You need to tell us where you go."

"I will." I thought of telling her all that had happened to me, but knowing she'd be upset, I said nothing. When I glanced at my wooden box – with the pistol – I knew I mustn't tell her about that, either.

She said, "Did you see...? Those Germans have gone. And the Russians are back."

I nodded.

"There was terrible fighting on the street. Bullets everywhere. People were killed. Not just soldiers. Homes destroyed. Did you see any of that?"

"Yes."

"We were terribly worried about you. You must always tell us where you are."

"I promise."

"Pray God this will be the end of it," she said, then added, "but no one knows." She put her knife down and rubbed her hands. "It's treacherous to even walk about."

"Do you need me to get water?"

"I got it. That friend of yours, Raclaw, the lawyer's boy, his family is leaving the village."

"How do you know?"

"At the pump, someone told me."

What would happen to them? Maybe I should go to Raclaw and ask for the button. "Will we go?" I asked.

"We may have to."

"Where?"

She shook her head. "Your father will decide. East, I suppose."

"The bridge is gone."

"Then west. It doesn't seem to matter."

"How long was I asleep?"

"All night. Have you eaten?"

"No."

"I'll get you something."

She took out a loaf of bread and cut off a big slice. Then she got a tin cup, ladled some of her soup into it, and set it on the table.

"Your father is trying to find out what's happening. So many things ruined. Destroyed. Now come down and eat." She set down a tin spoon.

I climbed down. "Were you here when the Russians came back?" I asked.

She said, "We hid in the workshop. Then, when it got worse, we rushed out to the fields. Promise me you won't disappear the way you did. We were very frightened. We must stay together."

"I'm sorry."

"They say some of the Germans were killed but they carried them away. Which boys were you with?"

"My friends."

"Jurek?"

I nodded.

She pursed her lips and then said, "He's wild. Keep away from him."

I ate some soup and bread, which made me feel better.

"You need to talk to your father. He should be home soon."

But as soon as I finished eating, I said, "I'll be

right back." Before she could say anything, I ran out through the front door and made my way to the main street.

60

Weaving among Russian soldiers, I headed for the pump platform. Jurek, Makary and Ulryk were sitting there. As soon they saw me, Makary shouted, "Did you find Raclaw?"

"At the ruins. He was shot."

"Who shot him?" asked Jurek.

"The Russians."

"Why?"

"You were there. The Germans made him go into the forest. Then there was that ambush. I took him home."

Ulryk said, "We went to his house. They wouldn't talk to us. Is he in a bad way?"

"I think he's all right." I climbed up onto the platform and took my regular seat. I said, "Remember that English soldier who was with the Russians? He was near Raclaw. Killed. I suppose the Germans did it. I made the sign of the cross over him."

Ulryk said, "Not sure you're allowed to do that."

"Well, I did."

"Raclaw's lucky," said Makary. "A lot of soldiers died here. It was scary. My family ran away and hid."

"So did mine," I said.

Jurek said, "The Russians came in one side and the Germans went out the other. It had nothing to do with us. Just them fighting. See what happened to the bridge?"

I said, "When Raclaw and I got back, we had to wade across."

Jurek said, "They blew it up. Just like that."

Ulryk turned to me. "Did you hear? Drugi died."

No one spoke until I said, "I liked him."

"I hope somebody killed that Austrian soldier," said Makary.

Ulryk asked, "You think the Germans will come back?"

I almost said, "Ask Raclaw's father." I didn't.

"People say so," said Makary. "I don't want to be around."

I said, "My mother told me Raclaw's family is leaving."

For a moment, I thought again of telling them what Raclaw had said about his father, that it was him who told the Germans that the Russians were leaving. That what he told them made the aeroplane come.

"Father Stanislaw is praying that all the soldiers go," said Ulryk.

"Hope God listens," said Makary.

"He must be busy," said Ulryk.

We sat still, everybody caught up in their own thoughts, until Jurek pulled out the Austrian button he had taken from the dead soldier's cap. "Then I guess I won," he said, and held the button out in the palm of his hand.

"Won what?" said Ulryk.

"Button contest."

It was as if I'd been punched. "No, you didn't," I said. "Raclaw has the best button. It's English," I described it.

Makary said, "Sounds great."

"How'd he get it?" Jurek said.

"Don't know," I lied.

Jurek said, "But he isn't here. Can't win unless he shows it to us."

Wishing I had kept the button, I hated that we

were still talking about the contest. To change the subject, I said, "Anyone know what happened to Wojtex?"

"Don't know," said Makary.

Jurek turned to me, "Just don't think you've won."

"What are you talking about?" I said.

"You said Raclaw got an English button. But he isn't here, so my Austrian button is still best. Or, maybe Wojtex got something better."

I said, "The contest is over."

"Isn't," insisted Jurek. "The rules. Contest goes on for another day. Only fair. Have to find out about Wojtex. Besides, you see those soldiers with red trousers? French. They came with the Russians. I bet their buttons are good."

Frustrated, I blurted out: "Forget buttons. I got something better." Soon as I said it, I was sorry I spoke.

"What?" demanded Jurek.

"Nothing."

"Come on," said Jurek. "You have to tell. Once you start, you're not allowed to go back."

Jurek invented rules faster than any human being in the world. And they were always about what he wanted.

"Not telling."

"Then don't say you got something better," said Jurek. "Means you're a liar. The contest goes on one more day. Otherwise I win."

I shook my head.

Makary poked me. "Say what you got."

I shook my head again.

Ulryk said, "It's a sin not to tell the truth."

"Yeah," Makary pushed. "What?"

Jurek gave my leg a hard swat. I waited a moment, feeling their eyes on me. Then I said, "Remember that English soldier?"

"The one you said was killed?"

"Was… Well … I got his pistol."

"*His pistol!*"

I nodded.

"You telling the truth?" said Jurek.

"Just said."

"Where is it?" said Makary. "Show us."

I shook my head.

"Not fair," said Jurek.

"Don't care."

Jurek said, "It's a lie unless you show us."

I continued to shake my head.

Jurek looked at me. "You hid it, didn't you?"

I kept my mouth shut tight.

"Where?" Jurek pushed. "Wait! I know. It's in that stupid box you have on your bed."

Furious Jurek had guessed, I kept silent.

Jurek said nothing more, but he kept looking at me with a grin on his face. It told me I'd better hide the pistol in another place. Fast. Wanting to end the talk, I jumped off the platform. "Going to Wojtex's house," I announced. "See what happened to him."

61

We ran to where the bridge had been and scrambled down the bank. People were using the old bridge planks to make a walking platform across the water.

We waded across.

Wojtex's father had his butcher shop on the main street. The family – Wojtex, his older two sisters, mother and father – lived on the second level. Though it wasn't a big shop, it was always busy. But when we got to the house, the windows were shuttered. Not only was no selling going on, there was a wagon standing before the door. Wojtex's father and his two sisters were loading chairs, tables, blankets.

Wojtex wasn't there.

We stood and watched. It was Jurek who called out, "Wojtex around?"

One of his sisters, who was putting a large kettle into the wagon, turned. She was crying.

She looked at us for a moment, her face showing pain, and said, "Haven't you heard?"

"Heard what?"

"The Germans said Wojtex was a spy. They shot him."

62

"*Shot him!*" cried Makary.

We stood there, open mouthed, shocked. For me it was no different from the time I saw the bomb drop on the school. I couldn't fully grasp it. Couldn't believe it.

"They really do that?" said Jurek. Even he was stunned.

Wojtex's father nodded and worked to wipe tears away.

"But ... why?" said Ulryk.

"He had a Russian button. They said it was a message. That he was a spy."

I said, "Because he had a ... *button*?"

One of the sisters nodded.

Ulryk made the sign of the cross over his chest. "God keep him," he said.

"We're leaving," said Wojtex's sister. "If the Germans come back, we can't be here."

"*Are* the Germans coming back?" asked Jurek.

Wojtex's father said, "My boy was fond of you. All of you. But ... please, it would be better if you went away."

I managed to say, "I'm sorry..."

"Yeah," said Makary. "Sorry."

"We liked him, too," Ulryk called.

Makary added, "And he wasn't a spy."

Jurek was, I thought. *Raclaw's father was.* I said nothing.

Wojtex's sister said, "Thank you." Weeping, she rushed into the house.

63

We swung about and started back across the village without speaking until I said, "This button stuff is over."

"Then I'm king," said Jurek. "I keep the cane."

No one said anything.

We waded across the River and without talking, headed for the pump. Once there, we sat in silence. I don't know what the others were thinking. I thought about Wojtex. And the village. When I looked around, with its smashed windows, doors, and bullet holes, it seemed wrecked. I was frightened.

Jurek said, "Just so you know, my sister's gone."

"Where?" Makary asked.

"That German soldier. The one who stayed with us. I don't know if she went with him or he took her."

I said, "You going after her?"

Jurek said, "She can do what she wants." Then he added, "Hate her."

I said, "What are you going to do?"

"Nothing."

"What about your other sister?" Ulryk asked.

"Don't know where she is."

"You going to live alone, then?"

"With the cane. Better that way."

After a few moments, Makary said, "Everyone's going. Won't be anyone left."

"I'm staying," said Jurek.

We were silent for a moment until Makary said, "Wojtex wasn't a spy." He slapped Jurek's leg. "You were."

"Button kings do what they want," said Jurek.

"We're *finished* with buttons!" I screamed. "Get rid of them."

"Only if you agree I won," said Jurek.

To my frustration, Makary and Ulryk said nothing.

64

I don't know how long we sat there, not talking, when we heard a rumble of horse hooves: it was a troop of soldiers on horseback coming along the street. The horses, having come through the River, were dripping.

These soldiers were wearing long black coats and, despite the heat, tall fur caps. All of them had belts into which were stuck what looked like long sheathed knives. Rifles hung on their backs.

Jurek cried, "Cossacks!"

Makary said, "Who are they?"

"Russians," said Jurek. "Their best soldiers."

There were about forty of them, and they paraded through town. People on the street stopped whatever they were doing and stared at them.

It was Makary who said, "Good. No buttons."

"Have to have them," said Jurek, "somewhere."

"Patryk's right," said Ulryk. "We should forget buttons."

"When you all admit I won," said Jurek.

As I watched the Cossacks go by, I noticed something stuck to their hats. At first it was hard to make sense of what they were. Only as I looked harder did I realize they were some kind of badge or insignia, a grinning skull and crossbones, the colour of brass.

Is it, I wondered, *a button or not?* Then I remembered Jurek taking the button from the dead Austrian's cap. If *that* was a button, weren't these skull things on the Cossacks' hats also buttons?

Get one of those, I thought, *and no matter what,*

I'll win. That would put an end to this stupid contest.

I glanced at Jurek, wondering if he had noticed the Cossacks' buttons. His face showed nothing. I couldn't tell if he had seen those skulls and cross-bones, because if he had, I knew he'd try to get one. I turned away, hoping I was the only one who'd seen them. I also told myself that if Jurek had seen them, I had to stop him from getting one.

"I keep trying to understand," said Makary. "Why would they think Wojtex having a button meant he was a spy?"

"Because they're dumb," said Jurek. "Anyway, now there are just four of us. Good."

"Not good," said Ulryk.

"Unless you're quitting," said Jurek. "Then there'd be just three."

Ulryk sat there, looking uncomfortable.

I thought about leaving and going home, but I was afraid Jurek would come after me and make me show him the pistol.

It was Makary who stood up and cried, "Hey, look!"

65

Two horse-pulled wagons were coming down the street, moving in the same direction as had the Cossacks. Holding the reins in the first wagon was Raclaw's father. He was wearing his black suit. Raclaw's mother was sitting next to him.

"It's Raclaw's family," cried Makary. "They're leaving."

Jurek said, "Heading for the German side."

"Where's Raclaw?"

Rattling and jangling, the wagons lumbered by. The first wagon had just passed us when some Russian soldiers stepped in front of it, one of them holding up a hand. Raclaw's father pulled hard on the reins, bringing the horses and wagons to a stop.

We looked on as Raclaw's father pulled some papers from his coat and handed them down to the soldier. The soldier appeared to read them, shifting from one paper to another.

"Bet you he's showing permission to leave," said Jurek. "Probably bribed someone. That's what you can do when you're rich. Get to go anywhere."

The Russian soldier handed the papers back to Raclaw's father and waved him on. The wagons began to roll again.

It was as they went forward that we saw Raclaw. He was sitting in the back of the second wagon, settled atop what looked like a heap of blankets. His left arm was in a sling. He had his cap pulled low, as if shielding his eyes.

Soon as we saw him, we leaped off the pump platform and ran after the wagon. "Hey, Raclaw!" cried Makary.

Raclaw, squinting, saw us, grinned, and waved.

"Where you going?" I called as we caught up to him and walked right behind the wagon.

Raclaw called, "My father said we can't stay here anymore."

"Why?" asked Ulryk.

Raclaw looked from side to side, as if uncertain about saying anything, but then he called, "The war is going to get worse. Besides, the Russians took our house."

"What do you mean, took it?" I said.

"Walked in and said we had to leave."

Makary said, "You going over to the Germans?"

Raclaw shrugged. "Just going."

"Where?" I asked.

"Not sure."

"How's your arm?" I said.

"Hurts."

"What did you do with your buttons?" Jurek called out.

"My father threw them away."

"Where?"

"Don't know."

"You ever coming back?" asked Makary.

"Don't know that, either."

Jurek said, "Drugi died. The Germans shot Wojtex."

"Shot him...? Why?"

"Said he was a spy," said Jurek.

"Because he had a Russian button," I added. "His family is leaving. I think they're going the other way. East."

By that time, we had reached the western edge of the village and the wagons began to move at a faster pace. We stopped and watched them go.

"So long!"

"Good luck!"

"Hope you come back!"

Ulryk called, "God bless you!"

Raclaw, with his good arm, waved goodbye to the four of us. We stood there until he was out of sight.

"I liked him," said Makary.

"He always thought he knew everything," said Jurek.

"Now it's just us," said Ulryk.

"Fine with me," said Jurek. "Makes it easier for me to win. You'll see. You're going to have to bow down to me."

66

Having followed the wagons to the west side of the village, we were near the old barracks. Long ago it must have been a barn. It was long and low, with a high, steep roof. Its white-painted walls were peeling. Its roof shingles curled with age. Along the side facing the road was a long bench. Soldiers were sitting on it. From the look of their uniforms – blue jackets, red trousers – I supposed they were the French. A few were smoking pipes, others cigarettes, their booted legs stretched before them. Three of them had musical instruments – the Germans must have left them – and the French were trying to play them, laughing as they squeaked and blatted.

The four of us stood and watched.

Makary pointed a little further west of the barracks. "Look over there," he said. The troop of Cossacks had tethered their horses and were erecting tents.

Jurek, however, seemed to ignore them, showing interest just in the barracks and the French soldiers.

"Why do you think they wear red trousers?" said Ulryk.

"I don't care," said Jurek. "I just want to see what kind of buttons they have."

"I'm not doing this anymore," said Makary.

"Because you're losing," said Jurek, who was already moving towards the Frenchmen. "Anyone coming with me?" he called.

Ulryk turned away. "I need to go to confession with Father Stanislaw." He hurried away. I was sure he was escaping.

Jurek said, "Patryk? Makary?"

"I suppose," I said, and started after Jurek. After a moment, Makary came, too.

We had walked a bit when Jurek said, "It might as well be just the three of us."

"Why?" said Makary.

"Ulryk is an idiot. All that church stuff. I knew it from the start: the button contest is just between us three."

Makary stopped walking. "I told you," he said. "I'm not doing this anymore."

"Patryk?"

"Not sure, either."

"Then you can both start bowing to me now. And you have to give me that pistol."

I said, "Just saying I haven't made up my mind."

"Same," said Makary.

Jurek went forward. We followed a step behind.

The three of us approached the barrack where the French soldiers were sitting. Jurek stopped and studied them. "See? Lots of buttons," he said.

I could see them, all bright and shiny.

One of the soldiers lifted a hand and waved at us. I think he was trying to be friendly.

Jurek said, "Come on. I'll show you something."

Instead of approaching the French soldiers, he led the way around to the back of the barrack. Once we got behind, he said, "See those?" He pointed to two poles, about twenty feet apart. A rope went from one to the other. "Know what they are?" he asked.

I shook my head.

"Forget? I used to come here to collect washing from the Russians. For my sister. That's a clothes line. Bet you anything the French will hang their uniforms there, too."

Makary and I said nothing.

To me Jurek said, "Remember how that night we got those Russian buttons from behind my house?"

"Uh-huh."

"Well, same thing," said Jurek. "I'm coming back tonight. Grab a button. You two want to come with me?"

Makary said, "What if those French soldiers see us?"

To me Jurek said, "You could bring that pistol."

"Why would I do that?"

Jurek didn't say anything, just looked at me and grinned, making me feel uneasy.

Even as we stood there, a French soldier came around the barrack. In his hands was a full basket of clothing. When he saw us, he put down his basket and yelled at us, waving us away. He even put a hand to the pistol at his hip, as if making a warning.

As we turned away, Jurek, low voiced, said, "I don't know about you, but I'm coming back. Tonight. Get some French buttons. No one will be here. If you don't come, I promise I'll get one and win. Because you won't dare to get one. But if you want to show up, meet at the pump when it gets dark. Late."

Makary had a troubled look on his face. After a while, he said, "I told you, I'm not coming."

"Patryk?" said Jurek. "You scared, too?" I didn't say anything. I was trying to decide how to stop Jurek once and for all. I looked towards the Cossack camp, wondering if I could get one of those skull and crossbones buttons. But the camp seemed too crowded. Too risky.

67

As we walked back to the village, I kept thinking about Drugi. And Raclaw. And Wojtex. What happened to them was all because of Jurek and the buttons. As far as I was concerned, I had the best button, that Russian cannon one. Sure, Raclaw had that English button. But he was gone. So right then I was the winner. But I knew Jurek would try to find a way to top it. I needed to keep him from getting anything better. Like a French one.

Makary said he wouldn't go along to get French buttons. That meant the contest was just between me and Jurek. With that thought, I had an idea how to stop him from getting a French button.

As we approached the pump platform, I stopped. "Need to go home," I said.

"You guys can always change your minds about tonight," Jurek said to me and Makary.

"Maybe," was all Makary said, and he headed off.

I waited until Makary left and then I turned to Jurek. "I'll go with you," I said.

"Great. Now the contest is just you and me." He gave me his best smile. "Best ever. Tonight, when it's dark, meet at the pump. Head for the French."

"Sure," I said, and started for home. Once, twice, I looked back. I saw Jurek go towards the river, in the direction of his sister's house. *He's really going to live alone,* I thought.

Certain he was going, I changed direction and headed back to the barrack, where we had just come from, where the French soldiers were.

When I got close, some of them were still sitting on the benches. I went up to them. I said, "Do any of you speak Polish? Russian?"

One of the French soldiers took his pipe from his mouth and said in Polish, "What do you want?"

I said, "A friend of mine is going to come back tonight, and if there are any of your uniforms hanging out in the back, he intends to steal some of your buttons."

"Buttons?"

"He wants some."

Sucking on his pipe, the soldier studied me. "If he's your friend, why are you telling me?"

I was ready for the question. "I don't like stealing," I said.

"He's coming tonight, you say?"

"Uh-huh."

"Does he know what we do to people who steal from us?"

I shook my head.

"We shoot them. Better tell your friend that."

"I will," I said, thinking, *Just like the Germans.*

I turned around, took a glance at the Cossack camp, and then headed back into town.

68

When I reached the pump platform, I found Makary sitting there with Ulryk. I sat next to them.

To Makary I said, "Thought you went home."

He said, "Changed my mind. I've been talking to people. You know what they're saying? That the Germans are going to come back. Chase the Russians and French away."

"How do they know that?"

"What people say."

"When?"

"Don't know. Soon."

"Think they will?"

Makary shrugged.

"I do," said Ulryk.

Makary said, "All I know is I don't want to be in the middle of it. Do like Raclaw. Get my family to leave, too."

"Which side?"

"Doesn't matter. Just get away."

I said, "What about the button contest?"

Ulryk said, "I went to confession and told Father

Stanislaw about the contest."

"Why'd you do that?" I asked.

"That's what you're supposed to do in confession. Father said taking those buttons was wrong. Didn't matter that they were small. He said, 'Small leads to big.' Said it was stealing. A sin. If I kept doing it, he said he wouldn't help me become a priest. So I'm quitting. I already threw my buttons into the river. Besides, Father Stanislaw might be leaving. If he does, I'm going with him."

I said, "Jurek won't stop. He's going to be king."

"Not for me," said Ulryk.

We sat there for a few moments, but then Ulryk got up and walked away. Just left. He didn't say anything.

Makary and I remained where we were.

"Just so you know," said Makary, "I changed my mind: I'm going with Jurek tonight."

69

"How come?" I said.

"I can't stand the idea of Jurek being king. Can

you? I hate it when he calls me scared. Don't worry. I'll go after buttons just this last time. Get the best and beat Jurek. You know how fast I run. After that, I'm finished."

"Don't," I said.

"Why?"

I was afraid to say what I'd done at the barracks. Or what the French soldier told me. All I said was, "It won't be safe. Don't."

"You're just saying that so *you* can win."

"Told you," I said, "I'm not going. And those French soldiers saw us hanging around back there. The one who told us to leave had a gun. They'll be on the lookout. Remember what happened to Wojtex."

"You tell that to Jurek?"

"He was there."

Makary shook his head. "You're trying to fix it so you go by yourself."

"Told you, I'm not going!"

"Well, I am. You can be scared. I'm not."

Stymied, I sat there. The two of us didn't say anything more. All we did was watch the villagers and people going about their business. It wasn't the way it used to be: everything moved slower, as if people were dragging invisible rocks. We also saw more people in wagons, possessions piled up, leaving. Others were going with sacks on their backs. It was as if the village was shrinking, disappearing.

We might have stayed there an hour. In all that time, Makary and I didn't talk. Just watched. Then I said, "You think the Russians know about the Germans coming back?"

Makary shrugged and stood up. "I'm heading home. But I'm going with Jurek tonight. You coming or not?"

I shook my head.

"Fine." He headed away.

I sat there for a while, trying to decide what to do. Then I pushed off and went home, knowing I needed to get rid of that pistol. I went in through the front door. My mother was in the kitchen. She said, "That friend of yours, Jurek, was just looking for you."

"Here?"

She nodded.

"What did he want?"

"Didn't say. He was waiting here when I got back from the market. Without the bridge, it took a lot longer. And the lines at the market are very long. People keep saying the Germans are coming back. Everyone is frightened. They're fleeing."

"You saying Jurek was here, alone, when you came home?"

She nodded. "He left soon as I got back. I want you to tell him he's not welcome here." I looked at her and then climbed halfway up to my sleeping shelf. Standing on the ladder, I pulled over my wooden box and flipped the lid open. The pistol was gone.

70

My parents and I sat around the kitchen table.

My father said, "I've decided; we have to leave."

"Why?" I asked.

"The village is being destroyed. And they say the Germans will be back. There will be nothing left."

"Where will we go?"

"With the bridge down, going west will be easiest. I'll bring my tools. There will always be wheels to fix, somewhere."

"We must stay together," my mother said.

"On the road west," said my father, "there are mile markers. If we become separated, wait at the fifth

216

marker. Understand. The fifth. That should be safe. Wait two days."

"Then what?" I asked.

"We'll go on," said my father.

71

I worked with my father for most of that afternoon, deciding which of his tools to take. We didn't talk much, and I didn't think a lot about what I was doing. Instead, I kept worrying about Jurek and how he had taken the pistol. Did he just take it, I kept asking myself, or was he intending to use it?

72

That night I told my parents I wanted to say goodbye to my friends. "I might not see them again."

"Come right back," my mother said. I went out.

The evening was much like the night when I went behind Jurek's house and got that first button. No clouds or smoke, so the moon was brighter, which let me see a good bit more. Some stars were out, too. When I reached the main street, no one was about, not even Russian soldiers. The abandoned, wrecked houses were dark and lifeless. Even the tavern was closed. The village felt hollow.

When I turned towards the pump, I saw one person sitting there. I assumed it was Jurek. That made me stop. I had decided not to tell him that I'd warned the French soldier that he might show up. But as I stood there, I changed my mind. If something bad happened to him, it would be my fault. I'd remind him about the French soldier's warning. Then Jurek could decide for himself if he wanted to go or not.

But as I drew closer to the pump, I realized it wasn't Jurek sitting there, but Makary.

"Where's Jurek?" I asked, trying to sound casual as I took my place on the platform.

"No idea."

"You been waiting long?"

"Some."

"Why you here?"

He didn't answer. All he said was, "You change your mind about going?"

I said, "I'm not going."

Makary said, "Then it's just Jurek and me. But I can't let Jurek win."

"Don't go," I said.

"Why?"

"What about that French soldier warning us not to. He had a pistol."

"Doesn't mean…"

After a while I said, "Where do you think Jurek is?"

Makary shrugged.

Deciding I had to stop Makary, I said, "Remember I said I had that English soldier's pistol?"

"What about it?"

"Jurek came to my house. Stole it from me."

Makary looked at me. "You sure?"

"Absolutely."

"Why'd he do that?"

"Don't know."

We sat there without talking.

"Maybe," said Makary, "he's the one who got scared. Ran off."

"Doubt it," I said.

"Then what?"

"He'll use it."

"How?"

"What makes you think I know everything?"

"You're his best friend."

"Am not. I hate him."

"Me too."

I'm not sure how long we'd remained at the platform when Makary stood up.

"You going home?" I asked.

He said, "I told you: just because Jurek got scared off doesn't mean I have to be. I'll get some French buttons and then I'll be king. We'll be done with this stupid thing."

"Going alone?"

"Sure. I know the way. I run fast." He took a step away, then paused. "Come with me."

I shook my head.

"Why?"

I took a breath. "I spoke to the French soldiers. They said if anyone tried to steal from them, they would shoot."

That held him for a moment. "When did you do that?"

"After we were there, I went back. Told them someone might come."

Makary studied me. Then he said, "I don't believe you. First you said Jurek took that pistol. Then that the French would do something. You're trying to scare me off. Just like Jurek. Make yourself the winner. I'm going. You don't have to."

"Don't go!"

"You know what?" he yelled. "I hate this button business."

"Then why you doing it?"

"Told you. Because I hate Jurek. I don't want to have him lording over me."

"Pay no attention to him!" I shouted back. But Makary was already walking down the street, going west.

"Don't do it," I shouted. "Don't!"

He kept going.

73

I watched him go, then fell into wondering where Jurek was. It wasn't like him not to show up. I had a feeling that something was going on that I didn't understand. Makary was just about out of sight when I leaped off the platform and began to follow him, though by then he wasn't much more than a dark shape.

No one else was on the road. If I hadn't known it was Makary up ahead, I'd have no idea who he was. Still, his shape was enough to allow me to keep in step. He was walking slowly, and as far as I could tell, he never looked back, so I'm sure he didn't see me.

It was when he drew near the old barracks that he stopped. I supposed he was trying to decide what to do. I was hoping he was changing his mind. I considered calling out, but there was some light inside the building that looked like candles. If there were French soldiers on guard, things might go badly for him, and me.

I stepped off the road and stood near some bushes. A good thing, too, because the next moment Makary looked back. I saw his white face. I was sure he didn't see me because he turned around.

For a while he remained standing still, as if trying to make up his mind whether to go on or not.

In my head I yelled, *Don't go!*

Then I saw him move forward into a deeper darkness, towards the barracks, until I could no longer see him.

I crept forward and peered into the darkness

to figure out where he had gone. Seeing no sign, I guessed he must have already gone behind the barracks, where the French uniforms might be. For a moment, I thought I saw him again, but couldn't be sure. Then it occurred to me that maybe someone else was there.

Was it a French soldier?

Was it Jurek?

I waited, holding my breath.

A gunshot exploded.

Shocked, I took a few steps forward and saw lights move about within the barrack. Next moment, soldiers burst out of the building, some of them carrying lighted lamps. They weren't in uniform but I assumed they were French soldiers. Then, further on, where the Cossacks were camped, lights also appeared.

Now scared, I ran down the road, towards the centre of town, looking back over my shoulder to see if I was being followed. I saw no one. I reached the pump platform and, in a glance, saw that no one was there.

Wanting to know what had happened, I took my regular place at the platform, then sat there and waited, hoping I'd see Makary come running down the street.

He didn't come. Even so, I waited.

74

I have no idea how long I sat by the pump. I just stayed there, my eyes on the road. No one appeared. I kept trying to guess what had happened. I knew I should be home, that my parents would be worried, but I had to know.

At some point, I realized someone was coming down the road in my direction – from where the barracks were. At first I couldn't tell who it was. Then I realized it was a boy, but I still couldn't see who it was. I kept praying it was Makary.

I waited and stared into the dark.

It was Jurek.

He came right towards the platform only to stop. He must have only just realized I was there, because his face showed surprise. It was as if he had not expected that it would be me sitting there – as if I were a ghost.

"Patryk?" he called. It sounded as though he wasn't sure it was me.

I didn't answer but tried to read his face.

He said, "I ... I guess you decided not to come."

There was puzzlement and confusion in his voice. He continued to stand in place staring at me.

I said, "Where's Makary?"

"Makary?" said Jurek. "No idea. I thought it was him sitting here. But it's … you."

"Did you go to the barracks?" I asked him.

"Said I'd go, didn't I?"

"Did you see Makary?"

Jurek shook his head. "Before, he told me – you were right there – you heard him – he wasn't going. It was you who said you'd show up."

I said, "We both changed our mind. I stayed. He went. I saw him go."

Jurek stood very still.

After what seemed for ever, he said, "I didn't see him." Then, after a moment, he said, "But I got a great French button." He drew close to me and held out his hand. "Makes me the winner."

I kept studying his face, trying to understand what had happened. A ghastly suspicion began to grow in my mind.

Jurek stood there, his hand open. I could see he had a button.

Not knowing what else to do, I took his button and peered at it. It was about the size of the others we had got, brass coloured, with crossed cannons. Between and over the cannon was a ball, which had what looked like flames coming out of it. I kept my head bowed and examined it. I didn't even want to look at Jurek. All I knew was that it was a fine button and I hated him for having it.

"Great, isn't it?" said Jurek. There was a bit of a sneer in his voice. "Nobody's going to beat that. I've won, for sure."

Still clutching the French button, I forced myself to look up. I said, "I want to know what happened to Makary."

"No idea. Went home, maybe. Admit it, I won," he said. "That button is better than anything you got." He held out his hand. "Give it back."

"Won what?"

"The contest, stupid. I'm king."

"Maybe Makary got a better one."

Jurek said, "Yeah, well, sure. Suppose. Except … I didn't see him," he insisted. "Didn't see anyone. Though … maybe he got there before me."

"Until we find him, you haven't won."

He shrugged. "Fine with me."

I flipped his button back to him. He snatched it out of the air.

With that, I jumped off the platform and said, "I'm going to look for Makary. If I can't find him, the contest will be just us. Whoever gets the best button – you or me – wins." I started along the street.

He called after me, "Stupid! I'll wait here. Get ready to bow down to me. I've got the cane." He tapped his chest with something of his old bravado. "Button king."

After a few steps, I stopped and looked back, suddenly remembering, I shouted, "Did you take my pistol?"

"What?"

"You took that pistol, didn't you? The one I got from that English soldier. I put it in my bed box. At my house. You were there alone. My mother found you there. When I got back, it was gone. You took it, didn't you?"

He looked at me but all he said was, "No."

"You did!" I yelled. We stared at each other, but he hid whatever he was thinking. It didn't matter; I was sure he had taken it.

For the second time, I said, "I'm going to look for Makary."

"Do what you want."

I kept going along the main street. As I went,

I glanced back. Jurek was sitting on the platform, not looking after me but into his hands, at the button, I guessed.

I kept on, and as I did, I couldn't keep that terrible thought out of my head: *Did Jurek – thinking it was me at the barracks – use that pistol to shoot Makary?*

75

As I kept walking, dawn began to show itself in the east, all red-purple, the clouds streaky. It reminded me of that day when I saw the first German aeroplane. Next moment, that *clatter-clatter* sound came into my head. As always, it made me cringe. But knowing it was just me, I didn't turn to look up at the sky. Instead, I kept on, working hard to push the sound away.

I reached the barracks. There was a cluster of French soldiers gathered around the front. A few Cossacks were there, too. They were all looking at something on one of the benches.

I stopped.

One of the soldiers noticed me. He beckoned me over.

I went forward.

They moved aside. On the bench was a body. I recognized him right away: Makary.

A Frenchman, in Polish, said, "You know this boy?"

I drew closer, my eyes fixed on my friend.

The French soldier said, "Shot." Then he pointed to himself and the other French soldiers, but shook his head, as if to say, *Wasn't us.*

I nodded. I knew that.

Feeling ill and unsteady, I simply turned around and started back towards the village. I felt I had to tell Makary's family what had happened.

As I passed through the village, a few dishevelled people appeared on the street. I paid no attention, nor did they care about me.

Makary's home was on the other side of the River. Which meant to get there, I had to go past the pump platform. I was hoping that Jurek would not be there. But he was.

I wanted to walk past him, not even look in his direction. That's what I started to do.

"Hey, Patryk!" he called.

I kept walking.

He leaped off the platform, ran after me, and grabbed my arm. "Did you find Makary?"

I yanked free, spun around, and looked at his face. It told me nothing. I said, "He's dead."

"What are you talking about?"

"Makary. He was shot."

Jurek didn't react. I waited.

He said, "By ... by those French soldiers?"

"They said they didn't."

"Then who?"

"You," I said, struggling to keep from bursting into tears.

"That's crazy."

"You thought it was me coming. But it was Makary. In the dark, you didn't see it was him."

"You really are nuts."

I replied, "Because you had that pistol. You want to be button king so much."

"I am the button king!" he shouted into my face.

"You're not," I yelled back. "Your rules. Just the two of us. One more day." I kept walking.

"Don't think you're going to get one of those Cossack buttons and beat me. You won't! You're too scared!"

I continued to walk. As I did I began to hear that *clatter-clatter* again. That time it seemed so real, I whirled around and looked up.

Out of the early western sky three aeroplanes were coming towards us.

76

Villagers heard them, too, and in panic, rushed out of houses and began to flee in all directions. Russian and French soldiers appeared. Standing on the street, they began to shoot their rifles at the aeroplanes. It didn't seem to matter.

I raced for my home and burst inside. Seeing that my parents weren't there, I tried to guess where they could be. Were they in the fields? Had they fled the village?

I began to hear enormous explosions.

I ran out the back of the house and kept running. Behind me, the explosions kept coming, as did count-less rifle shots. When I reached a field of potatoes,

I threw myself down, my face pressed into the earth, hands clapped over my ears. It didn't help: explosions, gunshots, screams and cries filled my ears.

How long I lay there I don't know. A long time. I do know I waited until the explosions and gunfire had stopped and I heard nothing from the aeroplanes. But the cries and screams remained – the sounds of people hurt, wounded and dying.

I rolled over onto my back and stared up. It was daylight. All I saw in the morning's blue sky were white clouds. I took a deep breath and smelled burning. I sat up and looked towards the village. It was crowned by flames and smoke.

I ran back to where my house was, hoping it wasn't on fire. Since I was coming from the fields, I approached it from the back. When I saw the house, the roof was on fire.

I reached the back door, yanked it open, and looked in. Swirling smoke poured out. With a hand over my nose and mouth, I plunged through the workshop and into the kitchen, and then the bedroom. Not finding my parents, I kept going, leaping out the front door, and looked up. The roof fire was getting bigger. Worse, along our alleyway, other houses were burning, blocking my way.

I tore back through the house. Eyes smarting, lungs hurting, I went out through the back beyond the fiery village. When I reached the edge of the growing fields, there were many people standing there, just looking, faces filled with horror and dismay. Many were crying.

I made my way along the back edge of the village, looking for my parents, until I reached the River. Believing they wouldn't have crossed over, I headed back.

Most of the village was in ruins, and what was left was burning with sputtering flames. I couldn't believe the destruction. It was like the forest. It was gone. Bodies lay on the street. A few people were stumbling about as if they were blind, creeping along the edges of the street, like beaten dogs.

More people appeared. Some had found wagons, horses, donkeys and were hurriedly loading them with what few possessions they had. There were even a few Russian soldiers, rifles in hands. I saw people standing amid a ruin looking for something. I joined them without knowing what we were looking for.

Even as I worked, I heard the sound of galloping horses. It was the Cossacks – perhaps half of the numbers that had come. They were galloping down the street. Going east. As they came, a shot exploded. A Cossack fell from his horse. The other Cossacks – without pausing – continued on and plunged down the riverbank, and emerged on the far side. Once on the eastern side of the river, they kept going.

The shot Cossack lay still on the street.

Who had shot him?

Fearful for my own life, I darted behind a smouldering ruin and peeked out.

Across the way, out from behind some rubble, I saw Jurek emerge. He had the English pistol in one hand. He ran to the side of the Cossack and bent down. He snatched something up and ran off.

I knew exactly what it was he had taken.

Afraid for my life, I sprinted back to my house. It had stopped burning, but the roof was gone, as was one wall. The front room was scorched and ruined. I squatted down near the front.

I waited all day for my parents. It was almost night and they hadn't come. At some point, I went into my father's workshop. The fire had not touched it. I rummaged about to see what remained, what I might take. It was under his workbench that I noticed a piece of paper that had probably fallen there. I snatched it up. In my father's hand was written:

Where are you?
We have gone west
Will wait
5th mile
Follow!

I decided it would be safer to wait by our wrecked house until it grew completely dark, when the moon cast the sole light. Cold, I put my hands in my pockets. The reek of burning filled the air. That's when I felt the German button. I pulled it out. Gleaming, it lay in the palm of my hand. As I looked at it, I felt disgust and tossed it away.

I worked my way out of the alley and went out onto the main street, or what had been the main street. It was littered with rubbish and broken things: a bed, a kettle, an empty picture frame. Bodies still lay there, among them the Cossack who had been shot. Nobody had touched him.

The village seemed populated with shadows. When I looked up, I saw no stars. I saw no living persons. I assumed that everyone, if able, had fled. I supposed those on the western side of the river went west, those on the east went east. I felt as if I was the only one left.

Then, out of force of habit, I looked towards the pump platform. To my surprise, I didn't see it. Puzzled, I walked over to where it had been, then realized it, too, had been reduced to rubble. The iron tap, with its pump wheels, lay, all crumpled, to one side. A pipe stuck up, and I could see a trickle of water flowing out. It was as if the earth was bleeding.

As I stood there, to my amazement, I saw someone climb atop the wreckage. I recognized him right away: Jurek.

I'm sure he didn't see me.

As I watched, he held up his hand. There was moonlight enough for me to see what he was holding in his right hand. Something shined even in the meagre light. I had no doubt: it was that Cossack skull and crossbones button.

The other hand held the cane.

He held them aloft and then, not to me, not to anybody, he cried out, "Everyone! Look at me! I'm the king! Jurek the Brave! King of everything!"

I spun around and began to run along the road, racing from what had once been my life, praying I could find my parents.

I did find them, waiting by a mile marker. They

didn't even ask what happened, and I didn't tell them. They silently hugged me and then we started walking together towards a city whose name I didn't know.

AVI is one of the most celebrated authors writing for children today, having received two *Boston Globe – Horn Book* Awards, a Scott O'Dell Award for Historical Fiction, a Christopher Award, a Newbery Medal and two Newbery Honours. He is the author of more than eighty books, including the short-story collection, *The Most Important Thing*. Avi lives in Colorado, USA.